JURY OF SIX

This Large Print Book carries the
Seal of Approval of N.A.V.H.

JURY OF SIX

DAVE P. FISHER

THORNDIKE PRESS

A part of Gale, Cengage Learning

GALE
CENGAGE Learning·

Farmington Hills, Mich • San Francisco • New York • Waterville, Maine
Meriden, Conn • Mason, Ohio • Chicago

GALE
CENGAGE Learning®

LIBRARY OF CONGRESS CATALOGING-IN-PUBLICATION DATA

Fisher, Dave P.
  Jury of six / by David P. Fisher. — Large print edition.
    pages ; cm. — (Thorndike Press large print western)
    ISBN 978-1-4104-6975-5 (hardcover) — ISBN 1-4104-6975-1 (hardcover)
    1. Ranchers—Fiction. 2. Nebraska—History—19th century—Fiction.
  3. Large type books. I. Title.
  PS3606.I773J87 2014b
  813'.6—dc23   2014006524

Published in 2014 by arrangement with Dave P. Fisher

Jury of Six

CHAPTER ONE

The two men sat on their bareback horses, hands tied behind their backs. Ropes that had been flung over a solid bur-oak limb ended around their necks. The limb jutted out a straight and level fifteen feet from the massive trunk, making it perfectly suited for the purpose. Three mounted men and a woman with glacial blue eyes stared at them.

The horses, free of their restraining bridles and saddles, fidgeted under the two men, wanting to be off to the grass that surrounded them. One of the men looked wildly about, his bloodshot eyes bulging in terror. He squeezed his legs against the horse's sides in a desperate effort to keep him from walking away and thus ending his life a few seconds sooner than the riders surrounding him intended.

"I swear to God," the man cried out. "I swear we didn't steal those cattle. We found 'em and knew they was yours and was

7

bringing 'em back to you."

The woman shifted slightly in her saddle, holding the reins like an extension of her arm. Her leather chaps were worn black, smooth at the thighs; her boots, run down at the heels, held star-roweled spurs. A wide-brimmed hat that had known uncountable seasons of sun and snow covered her short red hair, which was now streaking gray. Her life had been hard and she had no sympathy for rustlers.

The MacMahon belief was like that of most westerners: if outlaws went unchecked, no one would be safe from robbery or murder. With little or no law to call on, westerners dealt with outlaws as they saw fit. Hanging was a proven deterrent to miscreants considering a future as outlaws.

Her eyes did not lose their intensity as she spoke. "If that were the case, why did you start them on their home range and drive them east away from the ranch? Looks like you boys are flat-born fools. Anyone who'd steal cattle and then take a damn nap on the same ranch ought to hang for stupidity, if nothing else. Want to try another story?" Her voice still reflected the brogue of her native Ireland even after three decades in America.

The man began to cry. "Please, Mrs. Mac-

Mahon, it's not like it looks."

"Don't snivel, I hate men that snivel. It is exactly how it looks. You were stealing forty head of MacMahon cattle and for that you will swing at the end of a MacMahon rope. You rolled your dice and took your chance and came up busted. Just admit you're a cattle thief and don't snivel."

She shifted her angry gaze to the man next to him. "Do you want to deny it too?"

The man shrugged, showing no fear. "We knew you MacMahons were a hard lot with no give-up in you. It was a chance we took, but like you said, we rolled the dice. I got nothing else to say."

Ita MacMahon nodded toward the man closest to the condemned men. "Send them to their maker, Rafe."

Rafe Baker took off his hat and smacked it smartly across the rear ends of both horses. The horses bolted, the ropes snapped, and then swung from the bur-oak limb with a rhythmic creaking of hemp against wood. The other two men sat on their horses, unaffected by the hanging, as they watched the bodies turn in the Nebraska breeze.

The woman glanced at the two men. "Randy, you and George take them down and give them a proper burial, then mend that fence."

Both men nodded their understanding.

Ita MacMahon reined the sorrel around and spoke softly, "Let's get back, Rafe; we've wasted enough time running these two down. Let's move these cows back to where they belong and then get on for home before Caden thinks we're lost."

Rafe Baker fell in beside her. He had ramrodded the OM for twenty of the twenty-five years it had been in existence. He was here when Ita's husband, Owen, was still alive, as was Aiden, their eldest son. He had come in as a hand when the ranch was still growing and had carved a lifetime place for himself, rising up to the foreman position. He was on a first-name basis with all the family; however, when among the men he practiced propriety and referred to Ita as Mrs. MacMahon.

The OM was over fifty-thousand acres of prime graze on the Niobrara River. The MacMahons had come in when the Sioux were still fighting. They fought them at first, and then made peace with them, as they did with the Ponca. The MacMahons were tough people who had built a life in a country that gave no quarter to weaklings.

The OM was known as just that, the O-M. It stood for Owen MacMahon; it was the brand and the name. There was hardly a man for a thousand miles around who didn't know that name and the people bearing it. Their word was their bond and their handshake a million-dollar contract. Anyone questioning either would suffer the consequences.

As hard and unbending as they were in facing the elements or their enemies, they were solid, honest people. They were respected by all who knew them and feared by those who were wise enough to think twice before going up against them. No MacMahon ever backed up or backed down from anyone.

No man was ever treated unfairly by a MacMahon. The hands got three good squares a day, a decent bunk in a bunkhouse that didn't leak, Sundays off, and payday was the last day of every month without fail. To ride for the MacMahons was considered a prime position, sought by every cowboy in the country.

Caden was now the elder son, and he managed the ranch. Although he was only twenty-five, he had the wisdom of men twice his age. He was honest in all his dealings, polite to everyone, but like all Mac-Mahons, he couldn't be bluffed or bullied.

Caden's younger brother, Bren, wasn't as

work dedicated; he liked to drift. He would appear now and again, putting his best efforts to the ranch, and then get the itch and drift again. Bren resembled some of the west's toughest characters who were mostly gone now. He was good with his gun and fists, but tempered it with the fun-loving humor of an untamed spirit.

The hanging of the rustlers had been the culmination of a day-long search. The missing forty head had been discovered by Randy Banks, one of the two hands who worked out of the southeast line shack. Randy was partnered with George Carson, who was making his rounds opposite of him. Randy was patrolling the southern ranch border when he discovered the missing cattle.

The cattle tended to break off into smaller groups and graze together. When Randy checked for a particular group, they were gone. His search revealed broken wires on a cross fence and a trail leading toward the ranch's eastern border. He had followed, thinking the cattle had broken the wire strands and wandered away. That was his thinking until he came across two sets of horseshoe tracks plainly imprinted on top of the cattle's when they crossed a sandy-banked stream.

The cattle had been driven off during the night and it was dawn before they were discovered missing. Standing orders were to never pursue rustlers alone; a dead man can't bring back stolen cattle. Ita or Caden were to be notified immediately if rustling was suspected. He followed orders and headed back to the ranch headquarters for help.

Ita and Rafe had come back with Randy, picking up George at the line shack. It was July and the sun stayed late, allowing for more tracking time. The rustlers had made the mistake of thinking they were safely away. Tired from their long night's work, they stopped and took a nap, not realizing the size of the OM and that they were still inside the ranch's borders. They woke up to three mounted and armed men and the unforgiving glare of Ita MacMahon. It ended at the bur oak.

Cattle rustling was a problem for ranchers across the length and breadth of the western plains. With the Indian forced onto reservations, the country was becoming a safer place for outlaws wandering about looking for trouble and opportunities. These weren't the first rustlers to steal MacMahon cattle. Very few had gotten away while others had been caught and hung for their efforts. Once a trio of rustlers had tried to shoot their way out and had died in the gun battle.

Ita and Rafe drove the forty head back to their usual feeding ground and left them. They turned to the north and headed back for the house. They were an hour out when Caden rode up to them. He grinned, "Wondered if you got lost."

Ita glanced at Rafe. "Told you."

"Did you find them?"

"We did. They never got off the ranch. Randy and George are burying them now."

Caden nodded. "Just thought I'd ride out to check."

The woman's expression remained hard, but her eyes twinkled. "We certainly appreciate that. We'd get lost for sure if you didn't nursemaid us decrepit old folks. We should get back to our rockers and our warm milk. Let's go, Rafe, I feel all tuckered out."

"Okay, okay," Caden laughed. "You made your point. Anyway, aside from your warm milk, I wanted to tell you that Smith is here from the Agency; he's up at the house waiting for you."

"You're the ranch manager, why didn't you handle it?"

"Because, it's the government, and they will only deal with the person who actually has their name on the deed and *officially* owns the cattle. He won't deal with me. I left him sitting on the porch. I know you don't want him in the house."

"Damn straight. I don't want that crook in my house."

"Then pull the contract, Lord knows we don't need it. We can get half again as much per head in Omaha."

Ita stared off to the north for a full minute before she answered. "Because, if I didn't supply the beef for those Indians they would never get fed. Everyone else passes off their old diseased cattle like Indians were so much human trash to be plowed under for fertilizer. At least I know they're getting decent beef if they're mine."

They rode up to the house with an hour of daylight left. Hyrum Smith stood up as they approached; he beamed a false smile. "Mrs. MacMahon, how good to see you again."

She gave the man a cold look with no return greeting. She hated Hyrum Smith and his boss, Wendell Adams, the Snake. Not because they ran the Agency, but because they were thieves and cheated the Indians out of the rations that were allotted to them. They grew fat off their graft while the Indians starved.

She looked across the yard to see a half dozen Santee men sitting on the ground. They had been brought along to herd the cattle back to the Agency. She stepped off her horse and walked up to the man with no friendliness toward him.

Smith repeated, "It's good to see you again, Mrs. MacMahon."

She unbuckled her chaps and tossed them over her saddle. "The order was for thirty-two head. We have them penned and waiting."

The coldness was not lost to Smith. He knew Ita MacMahon hated him, but what could you expect from an Indian lover. "Very well then, I will have my Indians herd them back."

Ita looked him in the eyes. "Every head had better make it to the Agency, and tell that fat toad Adams that he'd better not be filling his fat face with my beef while throwing scraps to the Indians."

Smith stiffened. "I assure you, Mrs. Mac-Mahon, that every ounce of beef goes to the Indians."

"Bull! I know what the two of you are doing over there, it's no secret."

"If it bothers you so much, we can find another supplier."

"I don't think Major O'Connor would like

that. We kind of have a mutual agreement that the Santee should receive their fair allotment. Someone else might be more agreeable to doing business with you and the Snake on your terms."

Smith bobbed his head arrogantly. "Not to mention, you are both *Irish,* probably from the same potato field." He said the word like he had something foul in his mouth.

"I think you've worn out your welcome here, Smith."

"You can't wear out what you never had."

"You've got that right."

"Why do you love these savages?"

Ita studied the man's skinny face, spindly beard, and beady black eyes. He was an easterner with the typical contempt easterners held for the Indian, and most everyone else who lived west of the Mississippi. She hated what he represented.

"I'm not an Indian lover, Smith. We fought the Sioux when we first got here and that was a long time before the likes of you and the Snake slithered into this country. We eventually came to an agreement to live as neighbors instead of enemies; we could kill each other or get along. They're people, Smith, no better and no worse than other people and a damn sight better than the likes of you."

"What do you know about the *likes* of me?"

"I know exactly what you are; you're a thief and four-flusher. You're just like the lords and land owners in Ireland. They shipped people off to die to make a profit, protect themselves, and kiss the feet of the English. That is what is happening here to the Indians. I'm not an Indian lover in the sense you put it, but they are people, just as the Irish are people. It's the likes of you who grind them down to the level of worms."

Rafe sat on his horse, listening and enjoying every second. He was one of the white men who had come west first and built alongside the Indian and resented the intrusion of the gold-crazed fools who had flooded the Black Hills and the country around it. The first whites resented the dishonesty of politicians and their greed, which broke the treaties designed to keep the country safe for the legitimate settlers. Lies were the major cause of the fighting. Yes, at times they had fought with the Indians, but they understood each other. It was the likes of Smith and Adams that the early settlers despised for their weakness, arrogance, and greed.

Ita turned to the Indians sitting off to the side. She spoke to them in Sioux. They knew the MacMahons and respected them. They stood up and walked toward the cook shack. Rafe got a kick out of hearing Santee Sioux spoken with an Irish accent.

Smith did not understand the language of the people he controlled. "What did you say to my Indians?"

"I told them it was too late to start back tonight, to start in the morning. I told them to go to the cook shack and get fed."

"Does that include me as well?"

"No, you're not invited. I've never turned a man away from my door or camp hungry, but for you I make an exception. Besides, you wouldn't want to soil yourself by eating with savages and the filthy Irish anyway. It's getting late; give me the payment for the cattle and you'd better be heading out before you get caught in the dark. There are wolves and Indians out there who would like to catch you alone."

Pulling an envelope out of his pocket he handed it to her. Taking it from his hand, she counted it. "You count it in front of me? You don't trust me?"

Ita spoke as she counted. "No farther than I can throw you against a blizzard."

She handed the envelope of money back

19

to Caden, who stood slightly behind her. "Our business is finished here, Smith."

Ita pulled the chaps off her saddle and tossed them on the porch. She mounted and rode off toward the north.

Smith looked at Caden. "Your mother is a most disagreeable woman, maybe next time I *should* deal with you."

"You don't want to deal with me."

"Why not?"

"Because my mother is more easygoing than I am. If you had made that Irish remark to me, I'd have killed you."

Smith stared open-mouthed as Caden brushed past him and into the house. He looked up at Rafe. "What a family."

Rafe grinned at him. "They are that. I don't think that Irish remark did you any favors." He glanced to the west. "Be dark soon, you'd best be heading out."

Smith scowled at Rafe. "I suppose you're Irish too."

"My folks were Prussian and French. I was raised not to judge others by their name or color. Titles might mean something to you, but they don't mean squat to us."

Smith huffed indignantly and stepped off the porch. Pulling his horse's reins loose from the rail he mounted and rode out of the yard muttering.

Caden walked back out of the house and watched Smith until he was out of sight. "How long do you think he'll last out here, Rafe?"

"Oh, until they make him governor or senator, or the Army hangs him."

The sun was setting into a glory of reds and oranges brushed across the western hills. On a hill above the house, Ita sat on her horse and stared off to the northeast. Caden and Rafe watched her.

Rafe looked sad. "Not an evening goes by she doesn't sit up on that rise and look to the northeast. Always hoping to see them riding in."

Caden looked up at Rafe. "Do you think they ever will?"

Rafe glanced down at the young man. "After eight years? Not likely. Something bad happened out there, but she never gives up hope and I for one would never take that from her."

CHAPTER TWO

The young man rode casually down the dirt street eyeing the buildings to his right and left. He had been long on the trail and was interested in a drink and a meal that didn't come out of a saddlebag. He reined the chestnut gelding to a stop in front of a building that had a neatly painted sign on the front that read simply "Lilly's." He looked up and down the two stories of the building and nodded his head; this looked like a decent place.

Moving the chestnut the few feet over to the hitch rail, he stepped down and tied him off. Walking across the boardwalk he opened the door and went in. He sized up the room and wondered; it had a bar but nothing that looked like it served meals. A man dressed neatly in a white shirt, string tie, and garters on his upper arms was wiping down the bar in between pouring drinks. There were several men sitting around tables, playing cards. A couple of them glanced at him when he walked in and then returned to the cards in their hands. Since he was here, he might as well have the drink and then he'd find a place that could feed him.

He moved up to the bar and put his foot on the polished brass rail. The barkeep moved in front of him. The young man nodded. "Whiskey, Irish whiskey if you got it."

The barkeep's lips turned up in a smart smirk. "Sure, let me run it through a buffalo hunter's socks a few times and then it'll be fit for Irish."

The young man gave him a cold smile. "Nice."

Three men at a card table turned their attention to him and then looked at each other. One put his cards down and began to push his chair back.

As the barkeep brought out a bottle and filled a glass, a woman came up next to the young man and leaned on the bar, looking up into his weather-tanned face. "You have black hair; I like men with black hair."

He gave her an impish grin. "My brother has black hair too, you might like him as well." He knew now what kind of place Lilly's was and it wasn't beef and beans they served up.

She lowered her voice. "Send him around

some time, but you're here now. You drink a man's drink; can you do anything else like a man?"

He tossed down his drink and then continued to grin. He studied her brown hair, rouged cheeks, and painted eyes, eyes with a jaded cold edge to them. "I can rope, bust broncs, and fight Indians."

She slipped her hand around the crook of his elbow. "Come on upstairs and show me."

He wasn't going anywhere with her. He started to extract his arm from her grip when the man from the table forced his way between them. "Get away from my girl, Paddy. I don't want her contaminated by the whelp of an Irish whore."

The man never saw the punch that broke his front teeth, split his lips, and cut his tongue open. He slapped his hands over his mouth, stifling the scream of pain and shock that escaped it. Blood flowed from inside his hand as he fell to the floor whimpering.

The fallen man's two friends leaped from the table and charged across the room. They didn't see the anger in the stranger's eyes or the rage that turned his face mean and determined to kill for the insult. He caught the first one coming in with a left to the nose that stopped him in his tracks and rocked him back on his heels. A spurt of blood flowed over his mouth and down his neck. It was followed with a second punch that smashed his nose flatter against his face and dropped him to the floor.

The last man charged in and caught the young man with a punch that made his ears roar and knocked him against the bar. He bounced off, landing his own punch in the man's face. This one was bigger and more solidly built than either of the other two. He took the punch without slowing and threw another into the young man's face, causing an instant swelling under his left eye.

The girl had jumped back out of the way when the first punch was thrown. Fights in the room were not uncommon; she actually enjoyed them. She left the fighters and sat down at a table with another man to watch. She picked up the man's bottle from the table and took a swallow directly from it and put it back down. She smiled at him and he smiled back.

She was mildly irritated, however, as it wasn't the first time Matt Bolger had cost her a customer. She would make sure he paid her the five dollars she lost, even though it didn't look like she was going to get him anyway. She decided the young black-haired man was quite handsome and he could certainly fight, as he was giving the Bolger brothers better than he got.

The second Bolger stumbled back at him with his face full of blood. He received another shocking blow to the already broken nose that finished crumpling the cartilage in it. He fell unconscious to the floor a few feet away from Matt, who was still sitting on the floor dribbling blood from his mouth.

The big Bolger was still up and swinging, catching him with two more hard punches. In return the young man nailed him with four rock-hard right and left combinations to the face that stunned him. The young man with the black hair then grabbed him and threw him over his hip landing him squarely on a table that crashed to the floor under his weight. He hit hard and lay still.

With a curse muffled by the damage to his mouth, Matt Bolger jumped to his feet, pulling his gun as he stood up. The young man's hand snapped down on the butt of his Colt, yanked it clear of the holster, and shot Matt Bolger in the stomach. Bolger's body jerked backwards and doubled over like he'd been kicked by a horse and fell to the floor groaning. The blood from his bleeding stomach mingled with the blood from his mouth, making the floor a slippery red mess.

Catching a flash of motion out of the

corner of his right eye, the young man spun on the balls of his feet toward the bar. The barkeep was raising a club over his head ready to strike. He brought the Colt up and the barman froze in mid-swing, his eyes widening in realization that he was about to be shot.

The young man looked coolly at the barkeep. Holding the Colt at arm's length and pointed between the man's eyes he spoke calmly. "Now, what was that you said about Irish whiskey?"

Before the barkeep could answer, the outside door to the room opened with the sound of a man's boots moving across the wood-planked floor and a voice said, "Put the gun up, son."

Without moving from his position, he glanced to his left to see a tall man with a stern face but friendly eyes pointing a revolver at him. The man wore a large star on his shirt.

"Come on, son; don't make this hard on yourself. Hand me that pistol, hammer down, butt toward me." He snapped a quick look at the barkeep. "Beau, put the damn club down so he'll put up the gun."

The barkeep stepped back and lowered the club. The young man let the hammer down and reversed the Colt, handing it butt first to the marshal. The marshal took the gun and put his own back in the holster. He gestured to a couple of men behind him. "Get Matt to the doc and wake them other two up and bring them along to the jail."

He put his left hand on the young man's upper right arm. "Let's go, son. I'm going to have to lock you up until I can sort this mess out."

"I'll go along, but they started it, and that one," he pointed at Matt, "pulled a gun on me."

"Like I said, I'll sort it out, but right now I want you to come with me."

"Yes, sir." He went along willingly with the marshal.

They walked in silence to the jail as kids and adults alike ran for Lilly's to see what had caused the disturbance. They pushed in through the single door and tried to see through the two small windows. The men taking the Bolgers out pushed through the crowd, jamming their elbows into the heads and chests of the gawkers. "Get out of the way," one man holding onto a bleeding Bolger growled. The people parted to let them pass.

Entering the marshal's office, the lawman opened a cell door. The young man walked into it and the marshal closed it behind him.

"You ever been to North Platte before, son?"

"No, sir."

"Well, you sure made a grand entrance."

"What about my horse?"

"I'll have someone take him to the livery stable."

A few minutes later, several men entered dragging the two Bolger brothers. The marshal unlocked a cell at the end of the row with two empty cells between them and the young man. "Let's keep them apart; I don't want this young fellow finishing what he started."

The men dropped the battered Bolgers on the floor of the cell. They both had bar towels over their faces courtesy of the barkeep, although he had to be threatened into giving them up. The marshal locked the cell door behind them.

The marshal stepped out of the cell area for a minute and then returned carrying a wash basin. He opened the first cell door and handed the young man the basin. It held water with a washcloth in it. "Here, clean yourself up. The water's cold; it works better for swelling and closing cuts than hot."

He took it. "Thanks."

"What's your name, son?"

"Bren MacMahon, sir."

The marshal then looked at the two Bolger brothers sitting unhappily on the floor. "I gotta say, Bren; you really gave them a beating. Can't say they didn't have it coming, though. I'm going to ask around Lilly's and get to the bottom of this. I already got a good idea what happened."

"The one I shot called my mother an Irish whore. I won't take that from no man."

"I wouldn't either, son. I don't expect you will be in here for long." The marshal left the cell area, closing the heavy wooden door that separated his office from the cells.

The next morning the marshal came into the cell area. Bren was lying on his bunk; his left eye was black and swollen half shut along with a few scabbed-over cuts and red welts decorating his face. "I've got a visitor for you, Bren."

A heavily muscled man with gray hair and matching thick mustache gripped the bars with his two big hands. The young man sat up, looking at the scarred and broken knuckles around the bars and the hard look in the man's steel-blue eyes. He turned his head so he was looking at the big man with his good right eye. He grinned his impish grin. "Hey, Uncle Miles."

30

The man shook his head. "Brennan Mac-Mahon, why are you in my jail?"

"Your jail?"

"Well, it used to be my jail. I was the marshal here until I handed it over to my best deputy, John, here. I bought a saloon. Your ma would skin you alive if she knew you were hanging out in a cathouse. What were you doing in there anyway and it had better not be for the obvious reason."

"I'm no kid, Uncle Miles; I'm twenty-two years old. Besides, I didn't know it was a cathouse until I got in it. I had already ordered a drink when I figured it out, but since I had it, I might as well drink it, right? My Uncle Miles once told me it was a sin to waste whiskey. I was going to have that one drink and get out . . . honest."

Miles studied him, his hard eyes crinkling at the corners. "Hmm, okay. So, what started the fight?'

Bren jerked a thumb toward the Bolgers. "They called Ma a whore."

"Whoa, that was uncalled for."

"Not only that, but the barkeep, who was going to bushwhack me with a stick, said he'd have to run whiskey through a buffalo hunter's socks to get Irish whiskey."

"Well, that was really uncalled for. So, which insult started the fight?" His eyes

31

laughed, but his face remained stoic.

"Which do you think?"

"Yeah, a crack like that about Irish whiskey should get a man shot." Miles glanced at the marshal. "Yeah, that's him, John, my nephew."

The marshal grinned as he opened the cell. "I can see where the kid gets it from. Come on out, Bren."

The big Bolger brother jumped to his feet. "What are letting him out for? He started it."

Miles gave the man a disgusted look. "Shut up, Bolger. You and your brothers have always been trouble hunters; besides, MacMahons don't start fights, they just finish 'em."

"Well, he killed my brother."

John looked at Bolger. "Matt's not dead. He won't be digesting too well for a while, but he'll live. Besides, I got it from several witnesses that Matt started the fight, you two jumped into it, and then Matt drew on MacMahon here and got a hole in his belly for his trouble." John laughed. "And he really cleaned your clocks too. It's about time someone did."

Bolger sat down hard on the bunk. Crossing his arms, he glared at the marshal. "What do we have to do to get out of here?"

"You each have to pay a fifty-dollar fine for fighting and being disorderly."

"Fifty dollars! I ain't payin' no fifty dollars."

John shrugged. "Suit yourself; you can wait for the judge. He'll be back on the bench in a few days. Oh, and Molly says Matt owes her five dollars." He ushered Miles and Bren out of the cell area and closed the door behind them.

Miles turned to the marshal. "I appreciate your sending word to me about Bren."

"When he told me his name, I got to wondering, so I decided to check with you before I took further action."

"I don't see where any further action is needed, John. It's all pretty cut and dried. You know as well as I do the Bolgers have never been anything but trouble. Actually, I'm amazed they've lived this long."

"No, I'm good with it. Bren is in the clear." John then frowned. "There is a matter of a broken table though. Lilly wants a hundred dollars for the table that was broken when Bren slammed Bolger through it."

Miles hissed, "Yeah that sounds like Lilly. One of her cheap tables isn't worth more than ten bucks and you know it. If you want to get down to brass tacks, Bolger is the one who broke it, right?"

John grinned. "That's true, it was his person that actually broke the table."

"So, collect the ten from him for the table."

"I'll tack it on his fine."

Miles put his hand out. "Thanks again, John."

John shook his hand. "Bren wasn't guilty of anything except defending himself. I recall a lot of favors you've done for me. I owe you a couple."

Bren then shook John's hand. "Thank you, Marshal."

"Next time you're in North Platte, son, go to your uncle's place."

"Yes, sir, I'll do that."

Miles and Bren walked out of the office and stood on the boardwalk. Bren turned to his uncle. "How long have you been in North Platte, Uncle Miles? The last we heard you was marshalling in Wichita."

"I came up here about three years ago. I held the marshal job for two and then bought out the Buffalo Saloon; I've had it for a year."

"How come you never come up to the place anymore?"

"Busy down here, but I should get up and see your ma and Cade. Speaking of, how is your ma doing?"

"She's doing well, still tough as a bronc and twice as ornery."

"A woman in her position has to be. She needs to be three times tougher than the hands she controls and ten times tougher than the people who try to run roughshod over her."

"She's all of that."

Miles paused for a second and looked out over the land. "Does she still watch for them?"

Bren nodded and looked at the ground. "Yeah, she still sits out there every evening and waits until the sun goes down."

Miles shook his head. "Damn shame. I think we covered every inch of ground between Sioux Falls and the ranch. Come up with nothing."

"I remember. I was just a kid and went out myself a lot."

Miles changed the subject. "Anyway, I guess that's water under the bridge. Are you still drifting around?"

"Off and on. I head up to the place and help out in the spring and fall and then I get the itch. Ma says I'm just like you."

Miles chuckled. "That bad, huh?"

"No, Ma thinks highly of you. She talks about how you helped them get the ranch started, but your spirit was too restless to stay put. I guess I'm the same, except it's nothing like when you were my age. It's all changing too fast. There's no more Indians to fight, no buffalo left, you can't even shoot a man no more without the law coming for you. I wish I had lived in your time."

Miles smiled, thinking back. "Those were high times all right." He looked into Bren's battered face. "You would have done to take along, Bren."

"Thanks. That means a lot coming from you."

"So, where were you coming from and going to?"

"I had passed through Julesburg and Ogallala, and then stopped here on my way home. I'm still heading for home."

"Come on, I'll buy you breakfast."

The two sat in a café eating and catching up on the news of the past few years. When they finished, Miles walked to the livery where Bren's horse had been put up for the night. Bren paid the hostler and saddled the chestnut. The two shook hands and Miles promised to ride up to the OM soon.

The big clock that stood against the wall in the Buffalo Saloon was bonging out twelve o'clock when Miles looked out the window and saw the two Bolger brothers riding down the street. He laughed to himself when he thought about the beating Bren had given them. It was about time someone did. If this was back in the sixties or even the seventies all three of them would have been shot dead a long time back. He went back to his paperwork on the table in front of him.

He became lost in the figures on the paper. He hated numbers, adding, subtracting, ciphering, it was all part of being a businessman. It was easier when he was riding scout for the Army; he only needed to count his pay and ammunition then.

The clock sounded out two o'clock. Miles looked up at it and wondered where the last two hours had slipped away to. His mind moved on to the ranch and his brother. He thought of how Bren looked so much like Owen. Then he thought of Bren's fight and the Bolgers. He froze and cussed himself for a fool. The Bolgers were riding in the same direction as Bren. They were after him.

He scooped the papers together and dropped them on the bar. The man he hired to keep the bar was more than a drink pourer; he was his right-hand man, rule enforcer, and a trusted man whom he often left in charge. He was behind the bar washing glasses when Miles dropped the papers. The barman watched him and waited; he knew Miles was heading out somewhere.

Miles looked at him. "Gandy, take care of these for me. I'm going to be gone for a while, maybe longer. Watch the place for me."

Gandy nodded. "Sure thing, boss. See you when you get back."

Miles nodded his thanks and went out the back door to the small stable where he kept his horse. He saddled him, grabbed the saddlebags, and headed up the back stairway that led to his living quarters. He made up a bedroll and put food and ammunition in the bags. He grabbed his Winchester, buckled on his Colt, and was back at the horse in a matter of minutes. He headed down the back alley at a lope and hit a gallop at the edge of town.

Bren had pointed the chestnut to the northeast. His plan was to pass through Broken Bow and ride on to the Niobrara and the ranch. He had been keeping at an easy walk, in no hurry, just drifting in a homeward direction. He thought about his fight and the shooting with the Bolgers. He realized with a start that it was some of the same action his uncle had known. He felt that he had shared, if for only a few minutes, what Miles must have known in those days.

The chestnut was just splashing out of a narrow creek when he heard a big hornet zip past his ear; instinctively he swatted at it. At the same time, he heard the report from a rifle. A second hornet whizzed by his head followed by a rifle report. Suddenly he realized those were not hornets, they were bullets. Spurring the chestnut into a gallop, he made for a dense grove of trees a hundred yards away.

He reined the horse back and forth, running in a curving pattern and never staying in a straight line for more than a few feet. The rifle reports continued to follow him. He had no idea who was shooting at him, but he wasn't about to waste time looking around and wondering. When he got into the trees, he'd take a look.

At his casual pace he had only put a few miles between him and North Platte. He hadn't been thinking about danger and almost paid the price for his carelessness. He recalled Miles telling him that in his day no man ever lived long who rode casually. You kept all your senses working all the time and you developed a sixth sense that warned you of unseen dangers. He had better start practicing that, maybe things weren't as tame as he thought they were.

He aimed the chestnut between two big trees and broke into the wooded cover just as a bullet smacked into the tree next to him. Moving deeper into the trees, he knew he had to stay in this cover and fight. If he broke through them to the open country beyond and kept riding, one of those bullets was sure to find him. Aside from that he wanted to know who was trying to kill him.

Jumping out of the saddle, he tied the horse to a sapling behind a wall of tree trunks. Grabbing his rifle out of the scabbard, he ran to his left. He needed to put some distance between himself and his horse as he didn't want to be set on foot by a stray bullet killing the horse. He also loved that horse and wouldn't endanger him.

He moved in a crouch as bullets cut through the woods searching him out. He slid in behind a tree with a three-foot-wide trunk. He lay flat on his belly and looked back the way he had come. He saw four riders approaching the trees with rifles raised and ready to shoot. He studied them, trying to figure out what their problem was with him.

When they got close enough, he recognized two of them as the Bolger brothers he had had the fight with. Obviously they had paid the fines, got released, and came right for him. It looked like they picked up a couple of friends along the way. Well, enough was enough; he didn't need to spend the rest of his life looking over his shoulder for a Bolger.

Thumbing back the hammer on the Winchester, he lined the sights up with one of the Bolgers and squeezed the trigger. The rifle bucked and the man jerked sideways and grabbed his arm with a howl of pain. Bren levered in another cartridge and shot again with no effect. The four men broke apart and rode back a ways where they dismounted and took cover in the tall grass.

Bren cussed his bad luck: one ineffective hit, one clean miss. The man's horse had moved enough to spoil a good killing shot. Bren laid there and watched the country in front of him. He didn't figure these men were good enough to sneak up on him; still he had to be watchful.

He eased his way back to the chestnut and dug a box of cartridges out of the saddlebag along with some dried beef. He snatched the canteen off the saddle and headed back for the big tree. He was glad to be in the shade of the trees as the day had turned hot; those others would have to suffer the full effects of the sun. That might cause them to call it quits, or if not, maybe cause them to make a hasty move. He wouldn't miss with the next shot.

As his eyes searched, he tried to remember all the things Miles had told him about Indian fighting. Not only had Miles fought the Sioux, but he had been down south fighting Comanches as well. Miles had said that, in a situation like he was presently in, you had to remain patient and watch. To move around out of impatience was a guaranteed way to get killed. If a man had patience, water, and ammunition he could hold out for a long time.

As he watched, he saw a head bob up where the four men had dropped to the ground. Miles had also said don't waste ammunition; don't randomly shoot like a greenhorn. Wait for a target and shoot it. The head went down and he sighted on the spot. The head came up again, but it was too small a target. If he waited, the man might grow impatient and stand up.

No sooner had he thought it and the man's body followed his head. He was kneeling and craning his neck to see. Bren squeezed the trigger and was satisfied to hear the solid thump of the bullet hitting a solid object. The man fell over. There was a quick volley of gunfire that rained leaves and sticks on him. He moved from that spot and took up another prone position where he could see out to the grassland.

A fly buzzed around his head as the minutes ticked away. There was no more movement from the grass. He had no way of telling the time except by the position of the sun, and the cover of the trees hid it from him. From the shadows, it looked like it was heading into late afternoon.

Turning his head to look up at the blue sky filtered by the leaves and branches, he caught a movement out of the corner of his eye. He turned his head slowly to watch. It came again; it was a man sneaking in through the opposite side of the grove. He moved his eyes to check all around and didn't see anyone else. He slowly turned on his stomach to face the man. He aimed for an opening in the trees where he thought the man would pass and wasn't disappointed. The man's white shirt appeared in the opening and Bren fired. A grunt and a groan were followed by the sound of a large object falling. Again the trees were sprayed with gunfire.

Looking back, he could see three of his attackers' horses grazing in the grass. The land turned silent again and another round of waiting began. He was taking a drink from the canteen when several shots rang out. He instinctively ducked his head, but was surprised when no bullets whizzed through the trees. Another shot, then another, and silence.

A mounted man was riding toward the trees with a rifle in his hand. He stopped and called out, "Bren. Brennan Mac-Mahon, you can come out."

He recognized the voice, it was Miles. He stood up and walked out of the trees. Miles rode up to him. Bren grinned at him. "You got here just in time for the fun."

"I got two; there was another dead one in the grass drawing flies. How many were there?"

Bren gestured with his rifle to the trees behind him. "One back there. I saw four."

"Well, there's four horses, so I'd say four was all. Two of them out there are Bolgers, the third was an outlaw named Shorty Griffin. It's probably a safe bet that the one you bagged in the trees was another of their outlaw friends."

Bren grinned up at his uncle. "How did you happen to ride this way?"

"I saw the Bolger boys riding out of town headed in the same direction you had gone. I put two and two together and come looking for you. I just followed the gunfire."

"So, Uncle Miles, what do we do with them now?"

"I'll show you, get your horse and catch up theirs."

Bren caught up the horses and led them to where Miles waited in the tall grass. They threw each body over a saddle and tied it in place. They then tail-tied the horses together. Miles dug paper and pencil out of his saddlebag and wrote, *Marshal, North Platte. John, they tried to kill Bren and came up short. You know what to do with them. Miles.*

He shoved the note in the coat pocket of one of the Bolgers. "The horses know where home is, they'll head that way. Either they'll go in on their own or someone will find them and take them on in to John." He smacked the lead horse on the rump and they ran off toward the town.

Miles turned and looked at Bren. "It's just been your day."

"It's been different."

"Seems as good a time as any to ride up to the ranch and act sociable. Care for some company?"

Bren grinned at him. "Did you bring coffee?"

"Of course, only a greenhorn rides without coffee. Did you bring coffee?"

45

"Umm, I forgot."

"Greenhorn."

"If you're going to be like that, you can't come."

"Where will you get coffee?"

"Okay, you can come."

Miles tipped his head toward the trees. "Getting late, let's make camp in there and head out first light."

"Sounds like a plan."

Miles looked toward the departing horses carrying their cargo. He slapped Bren on the back, "Yes, sir, you'll do to take along."

CHAPTER THREE

Owen was twenty and Miles twenty-three when they were herded onto a ship in Galway on the west coast of Ireland. Their mother had died the year before in the famine and their father had been killed for daring to fight back. Michael MacMahon was a fighter and he bowed to no man and taught his sons to do likewise.

He had worked their plot of land, along with Owen and Miles, most of his life. The three of them continued to live in the stone and sod house after their mother's death. As the famine continued to ravage the country, the Irish landowners, working hand-in-hand with the British, began to purge the country of excess people.

On that day the soldiers had come to their cottage with the landowner to forcibly evict them from their home. The lord laughed as they were being physically removed from their home by the soldiers. Michael lashed out with a blow that gave the lord a bloody nose. The soldiers killed him for his insolence.

The two brothers were taken and loaded on a wagon with other men, women, and children bound for the western coast. As they moved down the road, the last view of their father was of him lying as he had fallen in the lightly blowing mist. The people on the wagon were broken, starved, and sick. Men were either angry or sunken in hopelessness, the women and children wept. They had heard that many were being sent to America and most knew nothing of the place.

The brothers had heard stories of the American frontier. That it was a free land where the only thing stopping a man from being anything he wanted to be was his own fear. No lords, no masters, no servitude. Owen and Miles knew they could go far for they had no fear. They had longed to go to America for a better life. However, with little funds such a trip was impossible, so they allowed themselves to be put on the ship for a free ride to America. Even so, it was with heavy hearts that they left their native land.

On board the ship Owen met Ita Flynn. She was Owen's age and had been separated from her parents and younger brother, who were on a different ship bound for a different port. She was frightened and miserable over the loss of her family. Owen took to her as a knight protector. He told her of his and Miles plan to go west and build a life free from lords and servitude. The weeks at sea bonded them together and when the ship put in at Boston they were married. The three of them together began their westward journey.

They worked at whatever jobs came along. Pooling their money together they continued to work their way west. Two years from their Boston landing, Aiden was born, a strong, healthy boy who thrived under the rigors of a family on a quest. Aiden was two years old when they crossed the Missouri River and came to the Niobrara River in a place called Nebraska. It was a land of water, trees, and rolling hills of grass. Buffalo, deer, and wild game abounded. It was a vast land and it appealed to them. There were Indians called the Ponca living in the area. They appeared fierce but offered no violence to them.

They met a man who had laid claim to a large parcel of land and raised cattle on it. He said the Poncas were easy enough to live with, but it was the constant raiding parties of Sioux from up north that were the real danger. It was never knowing when the Sioux would attack next or steal his cattle that had taxed his nerves to their limits. On top of that, he could no longer stand the isolation. He sold his land, with the cattle, to them for the four hundred dollars they had in their pockets. They had no idea how many acres they had bought as the claim was bordered by natural land points. They had become free landowners. They set to work building their new home and learning the ways of cattle. The year was 1855 and a second son, Caden, was born to Ita and Owen. Three years later Brennan completed the trio of MacMahon sons.

The three of them built the ranch together, working seven days a week for as many hours as daylight allowed. Ita packed the boys along as she worked until they were old enough to walk with her. All profits were returned to the ranch and its further development. They bought up neighboring parcels as the owners either headed further west or returned to the safety of the east. Within seven years the ranch grew to over 50,000 acres.

They fought the Sioux raiding parties showing no fear of them. The Sioux came to respect the two white men and the woman who lived on the river; they were warriors. In time they made peace. No violence erupted between them and the neighboring Ponca as they traded together.

Miles had put as much money and sweat into the land as Owen and Ita had, but he wasn't a man who liked to stay in one place. In Ireland he was limited to where he could go and what he could do. Here there were no limits and he didn't want any. He was a wanderer and would often take off for days at a time.

It was decided that the ranch brand should be an OM for Owen MacMahon. Owen believed it unfair as it did not include Ita or Miles. Ita told him that what was his was also hers and the name didn't matter. Miles said he would likely not stay so it was only right that Owen should run the ranch and have it named for him.

Miles went to work for the Army as a civilian scout after the Santee attacked the settlement at New Ulm, Minnesota. He stayed with the Army through much of the Sioux conflict that took place east of the Black Hills. He never asked for his share of the ranch or to be paid back. It was accepted between Owen and Ita that Miles would always be co-owner and was as much a part of the OM as they were. He was welcome at anytime and he made an effort to visit and lend a hand whenever he was in the area.

Miles and Bren had been back on the OM for a week. Miles returning to the ranch was treated like a homecoming. Ita had greeted them in her usual tough manner, but the softness in her eyes could not be hidden. She loved her son, and loved Miles as her own lost brother; they had shared joy and misery together.

She saw the healing bruises and marks on Bren's face and got the truth out of him. He held back on the insult directed toward her; he couldn't use that word to his mother. She had given him a mild lecture about ending up in jail, no MacMahon ever did jail time. She concluded the chastisement by asking if he had won the fight. When Miles assured her that he had, and against three men, she slapped him on the shoulder and told him he had done them proud.

They made no mention of the gun battle in the trees. Bren was thankful that Miles had neglected to tell his mother that the bar fight had taken place in a cathouse. However, Miles was quick to tell Caden and Rafe, who gave him no end of grief for teasing. He took it well and countered by challenging them to whip three men at one time.

Caden, along with Miles and Bren, had completed a riding circle of the ranch checking on the grazing conditions and taking a general tally of the cattle. They spoke with the hands who were working out of the line shacks and after a few days knew what kind of shape the place was in. It was doing well in spite of it being the first of August and a dry summer thus far.

The three were riding into the yard as the supper bell was being rung. They stripped the tack from their horses and headed for the cook shack along with the other hands. Ita came out of the house and was walking behind them when they turned at the sound of a horse trotting into the yard. The rider was Major Lewis O'Connor, in uniform, looking sharp and important.

Ita waved to him. "Come on, Major, you're just in time for supper. Tie your horse at the corral and get a move on before these hungry galoots eat everything, leaving only the bones and crumbs for the stragglers."

He smiled at her. "Just like a mess hall, the race goes to the swiftest, as does the food." He stepped out of the saddle, tied his horse, and joined Ita.

As they came in through the door, two of

the new hands stepped aside to let Ita and the Major move up in the line ahead of them. She shook her head. "Line forms at the rear boys and that goes for everyone. That's how it's done here."

The men stepped back in line.

The Major chuckled. "I wish we could teach that one to military officers."

"You lead by example, Major, that's how you earn respect."

"I hold to my original statement."

The end of one table was where the Mac-Mahons sat and it was always left open for them. The family sat down with the Major, sitting across from Ita.

Ita looked across at him. "Does your visit have a purpose or were you just looking for supper?"

"Actually, I have a purpose, but a soldier never lived who passed up a meal."

Miles swallowed a bite. "Amen to that Major."

The Major looked across and down the table at Miles. Ita gestured toward Miles. "That big tough man is my brother-in-law, Miles MacMahon."

Miles stood up and reached across the table, as did the Major, and they shook hands. "Miles MacMahon? I've only been here a couple of years, just since they put in the Agency, but it seems I've heard that name. Were you in the military?"

"Civilian scout. I rode with Colonel Sibley right after the New Ulm massacre and stayed on for several years scouting during the war with the Sioux."

The Major nodded his head. "That's where I've heard your name. You gained quite a reputation as an Indian fighter. Some of the older sergeants still talk about you."

Miles cut into his meat. "Those sergeants aren't paid near enough for what they do. I'd take a dozen tough old Indian-wise sergeants over a hundred spit-and-polish eastern officers any day . . . present company excepted."

"You won't get an argument from me on that. I lean heavily on my sergeants and depend on their experience. Did you know General Custer?"

Miles shook his head. "I was down in Texas and New Mexico scouting for Colonel Mackenzie during the Comanche campaign. I was at Red River and Palo Duro Canyon in '74. I took up the job as marshal in Wichita after that. I was there, and not with the Army up here, when Custer took it in the teeth at Little Bighorn."

The Major stared across the table at him.

"Red River was quite a fight."

"It was that, Major, it was that."

"So, you were also a marshal?"

"In Wichita, yeah, for three years. Then I marshaled in North Platte for a couple."

"You certainly have had a full life."

Miles grinned at him. "Not yet, I'm only halfway through."

"I take it you work on the ranch here now."

"Nope, just visit once in a while. I own a saloon in North Platte."

Ita broke in. "Miles was with us when we first came here in '55. He put as much work and blood into this place as anyone, if not for him, we probably wouldn't have made it."

Miles looked embarrassed. "You'd have made out just fine."

The newer hands who had not seen Miles before sat in silence listening to him tell of his life. He spoke matter-of-factly and not like a braggart boasting of his deeds. The young men, who had only heard the stories of the Indian fights and the lawmen of the wild cow towns, were impressed. Not only was Miles MacMahon physically big, he was a hard, battle-toughened man whom it would be wise not to cross.

Ita looked across the table at the Major. "You said you came for a purpose?"

"Oh, yes. I became so interested in Miles' life, I almost forgot. I will be bringing the new Agency man out to meet you as soon as he arrives."

Ita stared at him. "What happened to Smith and the Snake?"

Major O'Connor took on the look of a man very pleased with what he was about to say. "Well, remember those cattle you sold the Agency a few weeks back?"

"Yes, I told that weasel Smith to make sure they all got there."

"They didn't. He and Adams sold several head to a buyer at twice the price you were paid. They pocketed the money. We knew those two were stealing and working deals under the table to profit themselves. We had been watching them and caught them in the act. They were arrested and will stand trial before a military court since it was a military-controlled operation. Also, they were working under military law, which means they broke federal laws that carry a stiffer penalty."

"Can we shoot them after the trial?"

"I wouldn't mind, but unfortunately they will only get a prison sentence. At least they are out of the Agency. The new man is Harold Anderson and he seems a good man."

57

"Fine, bring him on out and let me get a look at him."

At the end of supper they headed back to the house. The sun was beginning to color the western sky as Ita turned from the house and walked up the rise. She turned her back to the sunset and scanned the country to the north and east. Major O'Connor studied her for a minute and wondered why she would turn her back to the spectacular color show to the west.

He walked up the hill and stood next to her. "Beautiful country isn't it?"

She continued to scan the country beyond her. With a resigned sigh she glanced at him. "Yes, it is." She turned and walked back to the house.

The military man stood alone feeling as if he had violated something personal. He hadn't meant to interfere and wondered what the story was behind her action.

He walked back down the rise and was met by the brothers, along with Miles and Rafe. "Come on, Major," Caden invited. "I've got a brand-new bottle of good bourbon, we were just about to take a sit on the porch and pull the cork."

O'Connor followed them up on the porch, still troubled, wondering if he had overstepped a hidden boundary. He sat down and was handed a glass. Caden held his glass up, "To the Irish." He grinned at Rafe, "And to those we consider our brothers." Rafe grinned and lifted his glass with them.

Miles looked at the Major. "You look troubled, Major."

"Please, call me Lewis."

"Okay, Lewis, you look troubled."

The Major thought for a second before speaking. "Mrs. MacMahon was standing on the rise in front of the house looking toward the northeast. I thought it unusual that she would turn her back to the sunset and look so intently toward the darkening horizon. I walked up beside her and I felt that I had intruded on something."

Rafe spoke up, "There's a story behind that, Lewis."

"Would I be imposing on a private family matter if I asked what it is?"

Rafe shook his head. "It's not a secret. It happened eight years ago. Owen was still with us, as was Aiden, the eldest son. Cade and Bren were in their teen years then and were at home here. Owen, Aiden, and me, along with a crew, drove five hundred head to Omaha. We sold them for a good price.

"Owen admired the Morgan horse and one of his dreams was to raise full-blooded Morgans. He had a line on a breeder up

Mankato way. We sold the herd; he kept part of the money with him and gave me the rest to bring back home. He and Aiden were going up to Mankato to buy the horses. I went back to the ranch with the crew while the two of them took the ferry across the Missouri and headed for Minnesota.

"A few weeks later Ita got a letter from Owen that he had bought seven Morgans: a chestnut stud, three black and three bay mares. He and Aiden were heading home with them. She got another letter from them at Sioux Falls. It said he would send a telegram from Yankton when he was coming across the river, which would put them home in a few days. That was eight years ago and no one has heard from them since Sioux Falls."

Major O'Connor sat in shocked realization. "My God, that's awful. I assume you searched."

Miles broke in. "We all did. We combed the country between here and Sioux Falls, but that doesn't mean much, that's a lot of country."

"Could it have been the Sioux?"

Miles shook his head. "I doubt it. The Santee were on the reservation and the other Sioux tribes were fighting in the Black Hills and over Montana way. They had problems of their own. I doubt they were even around to see them." Rafe pointed at the rise in front of the house. "She went up there and watched for them every day for months, but they never came back. She still goes up every evening to look, to hope, maybe to pray."

"So, I did interrupt something sacred."

"It's her time to be with Owen and Aiden. She knows they won't come back, but she still hopes."

Caden filled the glasses again. "We have never given up watching and looking. Something happened to them and maybe, one day, we will find out what."

Miles picked up his glass. "Owen didn't just abandon Ita, the ranch, and the boys and ride away; something bad had to have happened out there. Two men alone, seven magnificent horses, and who knows how much cash money Owen had with him. I'd bet my last nickel they were murdered for it."

The men sat in silence until Caden lifted his glass. "To Pa and Aiden."

Miles downed his drink. "And when I find out who did it, I'll kill him."

CHAPTER FOUR

The new day was breaking and promising to be August hot. Ita walked down from the cook shack and handed Caden a sheet of paper. "Sam needs this list filled; his larder is about empty of flour, coffee, and a bunch of other things. Take your brother and Miles into town with you and fill the order." She handed him a second list, "And I need this stuff."

Caden read over both lists and nodded. "I'll hitch up the wagon."

As he moved away Ita called after him, "Have Bren drive the wagon; if he doesn't have a horse and he has to stick to business, maybe he won't get into any fights. And, keep him out of the saloon."

Caden grinned. "Does that go for Uncle Miles too?"

"Your Uncle Miles can take care of himself; you just keep a tight rein on your brother."

"Yes, ma'am."

Bren grumbled all the way to Niobrara. Miles told him it was good for him, that it built character in a man to drive a wagon. Bren wasn't convinced, arguing back that a man on a horse was free to move about, and what if Indians attacked? Miles laughed at his excuses. There hadn't been an Indian attack in these parts in ten years, but if they did he could shoot from a wagon seat just as well as from a saddle.

Caden rode up next to the wagon. "I swear, Bren, you complain more than an old woman."

"Better not let Ma hear you say that or you might find yourself permanently nailed to this wagon seat."

"Ma ain't old. Just drive the wagon, little brother." He rode on ahead while Bren continued to grumble under his breath.

As they rode into the town of Niobrara, Caden pointed at the store and looked at Bren. "Start there, I've got some things to pick up for Ma."

Bren's tone was laced with sarcasm. "Oh, you mean the store? Do we really get our supplies at the store? Oh, thank you, wise brother, for pointing that out to me. I see now why you are the older brother."

Caden shook his head and rode on down

the street.

Miles tied off his horse and grinned at Bren. "One of these days Cade is going to kick your smart tail over this county. Well, I hear a glass of whiskey calling my name, maybe that's a beer I hear too. You have a good time loading the wagon."

"Well, that ain't fair."

"Who said life was fair? Look on this as a character-building exercise." He laughed and walked across the street to a saloon.

Caden continued riding down the street. His attention was drawn to a young woman sitting on a wagon seat next to an older woman who was wrapping the team's reins around the brake handle. The young woman turned and he could see her finely featured face framed by a light blue bonnet tied under her chin. Wisps of brown hair had found their way out from the edge of the bonnet and hung loosely alongside her eyes.

As she stood up and attempted to step down from the wagon her dress caught on the metal wagon frame and she fell from the wagon. Caden cringed as he saw it happen, but was too far away to prevent the fall. The young woman landed face down in the dusty street with a resounding thud. Caden jumped from his horse and ran to her.

The woman was attempting to push herself up with her arms when Caden knelt down by her side. "Are you all right? You took a nasty fall. Don't move until you're sure nothing is broken."

Her bonnet was knocked to the back of her head, revealing her dark brown hair as she pushed herself up. Tears were running down her cheeks. Caden helped her to a sitting position while several more men crowded around to see if they could help. She looked up at Caden, her face flushed with embarrassment and covered in dust and mud from the tears. Her dress was covered in dust as well.

The older woman was now beside her. "Josephine, are you hurt?"

She shook her head, "I don't think so."

Josephine looked at Caden, "Thank you for helping. I feel so foolish . . . I'm so embarrassed."

Caden smiled at her, "Don't be, we've all had accidents. Do you feel injured at all?"

She shook her head and smiled, "Only my vanity."

He helped her to stand and was about to assist brushing the dirt from the front of her dress, an ingrained habit to help, when he caught himself and jerked his hand back to his chest. The older woman smiled lightly at him and murmured, "You are a gentleman to assist, and a wiser one to know when not to."

He blushed slightly and nodded. "I will leave that part of the assistance to you."

After a minute of brushing and straightening the bonnet, Josephine wiped her face with a white hanky. She smiled at Caden, "Thank you again."

"It was nothing any western man wouldn't have done."

She continued to look at him, "Do you live here?"

With a jab of his thumb over his shoulder he answered, "We have a ranch up the river a ways."

"What is your name?"

"Caden is my given name, but everyone calls me Cade."

"I am Josephine Stanford, but I prefer to be called Jo."

"Pleasure to meet you, Jo; I'm sorry our first meeting wasn't under more favorable circumstances."

The young woman laughed. "Me too. Well, Caden, thank you again. You were most gallant."

"Yes, ma'am." Feeling uncomfortable with the praise he changed the subject. "Are you new here?"

"Yes, we have recently moved here. We came from Mankato. My uncle and aunt live in Stanfordville and encouraged us to move here. My father wishes to start in the cattle business. His brother, Dillon Stanford, is going to help him."

Caden nodded, "This is a good time for cattle."

"Do you know of Stanfordville?"

Caden shook his head, "No, I'm not familiar with it."

Concerned that Josephine was revealing too much information to a stranger, the other woman broke in. "I am Josephine's mother. Since we are new here perhaps you could assist us. We came in today to learn the town and where we can buy supplies. Could you direct us?"

"Yes, ma'am, I could." He pointed behind him. "Neil Barnett has the general store; everything you could want in the way of canned and dried goods, as well as clothes and hardware, can be found there."

He pointed in the opposite direction. "Charlie Snooks has the ranch supply store down that way. The ranchers began stringing barbed wire a few years back and he carries it and other tools." He continued to point out the various shops and stores.

Mrs. Stanford thanked him. "I believe we

will start at the store." She climbed back up on the wagon and loosened the reins.

Wincing, Josephine looked up at her. "I believe I will walk, Mother."

She smiled up at Caden and he took the liberty of looking directly into her eyes; they were hazel colored with flecks of green. She was an attractive woman and he felt his stomach tighten. "May I walk with you?"

"Yes, that would be nice." She looked at him coyly. "Maybe you could help us load the wagon?"

"Of course." He picked up the trailing reins to his horse and led him as he walked beside her.

Mrs. Stanford expertly pulled the wagon in beside the MacMahon wagon. Bren threw a second large sack of flour into the bed of his wagon and wiped the sweat from his face. He looked up to see Caden walking with a girl toward the wagon that had pulled in. He watched his brother as he walked into the store with the girl. He rolled his eyes back.

A few minutes passed before Caden came out carrying a large sack of flour from the store and put it in the bed of the neighboring wagon. Bren stood beside their wagon as his eyes followed his brother's steady pace. His look was incredulous as he watched Caden make repeated trips in and out of the store loading supplies in the wagon. Miles walked up to Bren with a grin and a match sticking out from between his teeth. Bren looked at him; obviously the whiskey was having a cheerful effect on his uncle.

Miles stood next to Bren; both leaned on the wagon and watched Caden walking in and out of the store carrying packages and sacks of dry goods. Bren spoke loud enough for Caden to hear, "Amazing how much energy a man can muster to load a wagon."

Miles' grin widened around the match. "Depends on the incentive, Bren."

Josephine came out of the store and stood watching. Miles gestured with his head toward her. "Now, that young lady right there would be enough incentive to make *me* load a wagon on a hot August day."

The girl looked at them. Caden dropped a sack in the wagon and turned to her. "Jo, meet my brother Bren and my Uncle Miles." They both tipped the brims of their hats toward her.

"Oh, I'm sorry; did I pull you away from your work?"

"No, they're just having fun. Bren would rather fight than work, and Uncle Miles doesn't like work at all."

Miles was still grinning. "I've spent my whole life avoiding it, seems a shame to change my habits in my old age."

Josephine smiled at them. "I see you are a fun-loving family."

"Yes, ma'am, we have our moments."

Mrs. Stanford came out of the store. "We are finished, Josephine." She turned to Caden. "Thank you so much for all your help, Caden." She noticed Bren and Miles watching the exchange and grinning. She looked at them crossly. "Can I help you, gentlemen?"

Bren shook his head. "No, ma'am, we are just in awe watching a man work like that."

She frowned at them and then Josephine explained. "Those two are Caden's brother and uncle; they have been teasing him because he is loading our wagon instead of theirs."

The woman's expression lightened. "Oh, I see."

"Mother, may we have Caden over for supper tonight . . . to show our thanks for his help today?"

"Yes, I suppose that would be all right."

Josephine turned her attention back to Caden. "You can meet my father and discuss cattle since we are all raising cattle."

Mrs. Stanford and Jo exchanged nervous

glances. Jo whispered to her, "Maybe he won't."

Caden sensed there was a problem concerning Jo's father, but he wanted to see her again. "I would like that fine, thank you."

"We live south of here. Follow the road along Verdigris Creek until it crosses the stream and we are the white house."

He helped Josephine climb back onto the wagon. "See you this evening then."

"Yes, this evening. I will look forward to it." She waved at him and then smiled at Bren and Miles. "He can help you load your wagon now." She waved at them and they waved in return.

Mrs. Stanford snapped reins to the team and pulled out onto the street and moved away.

Bren looked at his brother. "Have a rough morning?"

"Nope, had a pretty good one." He grinned at Bren. "I'd best get Ma's order filled and back to the ranch so I can get cleaned up and head on back here."

Miles took the match from his mouth. "Can't blame you a bit, son, that's a mighty pretty girl. Her ma seems to have some iron in her, best behave yourself."

"I'll be the perfect gentleman."

71

"She happen to say what her last name was?"

"Stanford. They just moved here from Minnesota, her father's getting into the cattle business. I guess her uncle is some big shakes down south of here, man name of Dillon Stanford from Stanfordville."

Miles froze with the match held in his fingers. "I knew a Dillon Stanford once. He was a no-account slimy rat. He was in the cavalry and was arrested for stealing." Miles shook his head at the memory. "He was caught robbing the bodies of dead soldiers on the field. He was court-martialed and served a few years in prison. He was a coward, but very dangerous because he was ruthless and a backshooter."

"Couldn't be the same man, not if Jo and her mother are any gauge. Sounds like he's been here a while, even has the town named after him."

"The Dillon Stanford I knew came back to Yankton after he got out of prison. He hung around the saloons drinking and gambling. He took up with a prostitute, a hardcase, mean as sin woman who liked to entertain soldiers. Her name was Kelly, but the soldiers had a lot of other names for her.

"The two of them were suspected of committing robbery and murder against travelers. It was never proved, though. Then one day they were gone; someone said he won a piece of land in a poker game. That was the last anyone ever saw of either of them."

Bren looked at Miles. "When was that?"

"In the 60s. Must have been about '70, '71 that he was last seen around Yankton."

Bren shifted his eyes to Caden. "If this girl's uncle is big enough to have a town in his name, you'd think we would have heard of him."

Caden shrugged. "Not necessarily. It's a big country and we haven't been over all of it. He might do his trading in St. Helena or maybe this Stanfordville is all he needs."

Bren looked down the street at the receding wagon. "Maybe." He looked back at Caden. "You have enough strength left to help me load?"

"Can't, got to fill Ma's order." He pointed at Miles. "You know, you haven't exactly killed yourself today."

"Sorry, boys." He twisted his right shoulder. "Old Indian arrowhead wound flaring up, don't figure I could lift a kitten today."

Bren scowled at him. "Then, you're in luck, we aren't lifting any kittens today so you can help." He grabbed Miles by the sleeve and pulled him toward the store.

"Come on, you can use some character-building work your ownself, you old whiskey-drinking Indian fighter."

"Oh, all right, but just this once. I'd hate to ruin my reputation."

Caden rode toward Niobrara late in the afternoon headed for the Stanford home. He had washed and shaved and put on his best clothes. He had to endure some more teasing from Bren and Miles; even Rafe threw in a whistle and told him he looked like a man goin' courtin'. Ita had smiled at him and said he looked handsome and a credit to the MacMahon name.

He followed the Verdigris road south until he came to a wooden bridge over the creek and beyond it was a white house. It was a nice piece of land with trees, grass, and water. Year-round water was vital to a ranch and the Stanford place had it. He could see a handful of mixed cattle grazing on a hillside, but no fences. He might want to mention the value of fencing now that more of the ranch lands were bordering each other.

He pulled up to the front of the house. Josephine came out on the porch and smiled at him. "Good afternoon, Caden."

He tipped his hat to her. "And to you, Josephine." He stepped out of the saddle, tied his horse to the rail, and loosened the cinch to let the horse rest more comfortably.

As he stepped up on the porch, the girl was still smiling. "I thought I told you I preferred Jo?"

"I'll make you a deal; I'll call you Jo if you call me Cade."

She put out her hand. "Done." They shook hands and laughed.

Jo opened the door and walked in with Caden following. He removed his hat and took a quick look around the portion of the house he could see. It was neat and clean with a sitting room off to the right and other rooms ahead of him.

Jo called out, "Mother, Cade is here."

Mrs. Stanford stepped out of the kitchen and greeted him. "Have a seat in the parlor, Caden. Arthur will be in presently."

Jo led him into the room where he took a seat in a chair. Jo sat opposite him and began making small talk. As they talked they heard the back door open and a man's voice joined Mrs. Stanford's. The footsteps proceeded toward the parlor.

Arthur Stanford stepped into the room. Caden stood up to meet him and was surprised to see that Stanford was not what he expected. He was accustomed to ranchers being muscled and hearty with weather-etched faces. Arthur was below-average height, slight of build, with a face that had been long indoors. His overall appearance was of a weak man.

He moved toward Caden and extended his hand. "So, you are the man who stepped forward to help my daughter."

He shook his hand. "Yes, sir."

Arthur gestured toward the chair Caden had been sitting in. "Sit."

Arthur sat in what appeared to be his favorite chair. "Josephine tells me you are into cattles."

"Yes, sir, we have a place up on the Niobrara."

"We've been here for a couple of months. My brother talked me into moving down here and raising cattles like he is. Maybe you know him, Dillon Stanford?"

Caden shook his head. "No, I don't know him."

"Well, he is quite prominent, but perhaps you are new here and haven't heard of everyone yet."

"Yes, sir, that's possible."

"I have two *hundred* acres here. I am going to be a big man in these parts; why with two hundred acres and the cattles I have, I will soon be an important cattleman. Between me and my brother, who has over a thousand acres, and several hundred cattles, we'll be important men in Nebraska. My brother also raises fine-blooded horses and he owns most of the town of Stanfordville. So, how big is your place? Can you compare to me and my brother?"

The first thing that struck Caden was Arthur's reference to "cattles"; no cattleman ever said "cattles." Aside from that, the question regarding the size of their place caused Caden to stiffen angrily, but he kept it hidden. No man in the west ever asked how much land you owned or how many head you run. It was the height of rudeness and arrogance to do so.

Caden was getting a creeping feeling that he did not like Arthur Stanford. He was obviously a city man that had not lived an outdoor life. There was nothing wrong with that in itself. It was his self-impressed attitude, common to many city dwellers he had met, that he found annoying. There was also something in Stanford's eyes, a shrewd coldness that left Cade feeling that what was on the outside of the man was not on the inside. A feeling he did not get from either Jo or her mother.

This man was not only ignorant of western customs; he was haughtily throwing the wrong terms around. Arthur Stanford was not a cattleman. Maybe he was a braggart running his mouth and trying to act like a big cattleman, but there was something in the man that made Caden believe the ranch was not his livelihood, that there was something else he did.

He wanted to teach Arthur Stanford a thing or two about manners, but he was a guest in their home. He must remain polite even if smoke was coming out of his ears. He also thought of Jo and how he wanted to court her. Starting a fight with her father on the first visit would doom that.

Mrs. Stanford had walked quietly to the entryway of the room and listened. Caden glanced at her and saw anger in her expression. He cast a quick look at Jo, who sat with a horrified look in her eyes, and her face was red with embarrassment. Arthur sat back in his chair with a self-satisfied expression.

Caden shrugged. "We don't have two hundred acres."

Arthur beamed with triumph that he had bested his daughter's caller. "Maybe my brother can give you some advice on raising cattles. He has certainly helped me."

"Thank you, I'll have to look him up."

He was glad when Mrs. Stanford called

them to dinner. The visit had become strained and uncomfortable. They filed into the kitchen and took their places at the table. Mrs. Stanford was obviously annoyed with her husband, Jo was embarrassed, and Arthur sat with the haughty demeanor of a self-impressed braggart.

They ate for several minutes in silence before Arthur broke it. "Say, Caden, what do you think of this fencing business out here? My brother thinks it is necessary, I'm not so sure."

Caden pushed down his annoyance and held his tone neutral. "Land's filling up, you can't have everyone's cattle mixing together. We fenced off our place a few years back."

"Yes, but fencing two *hundred* acres is quite a job, not to mention expensive."

"I could help you if you want, show you what we did."

"We have fences in Minnesota too; I know how to build a fence. Besides, my brother has hired men who can help if I need it, which I don't, because I know what I am doing when it comes to cattles."

The women looked even more uncomfortable. Mrs. Stanford looked at her husband and spoke with irritation. "I think we have talked about your brother and cattle enough, Arthur."

The remainder of the dinner was spent in awkward silence with husband and wife glaring at each other as they ate. When they had finished eating, Arthur leaned back in his chair. "I understand there are some cattle-stealing problems around here, but I doubt it is as bad as all that."

Caden looked at him. "It's as bad as all that."

"Have you had any cattle-theft problems at your place? Maybe not, if your place is small and only has a few cattles."

Mrs. Stanford locked an angry glare on her husband and held it until he looked at her and glared defiantly back at her.

Caden answered, "We've had our share."

"Really? How do you deal with it, call the sheriff?"

"There is no sheriff around here. We take care of it ourselves, like we always have."

Arthur looked at Caden with a doubting expression. "Oh, really, how is that?"

Caden looked the man straight in the eyes. His voice was frigid. "We hang 'em."

Arthur's face blanched whiter. His eyes widened and fear flashed across them. "You take the law in your own hands?"

"This isn't the east where there's a lawman on every corner. We do what needs doing. If you don't deal harshly with outlaws out here they will think you're weak and not only wipe you out, but murder you to boot."

"Well, I hardly see that to be the case."

Caden needed to change the subject before he strangled the man. "You came from Mankato; do you know a man who raises pureblood Morgan horses up there?"

The question set Arthur back and speechless for a single second before regaining his arrogant pose. "No, I can't say that I do. Why?"

"Because my father and brother went up there to buy Morgans several years back from a breeder in Mankato. You being from there I'd think you would have heard of someone like that."

"I wasn't in the livestock business back then, so I wouldn't know."

For the first time Jo was able to break into the conversation. "Morgans are such beautiful horses. Do you raise Morgans now, Cade?"

Caden held his eyes on Arthur as he answered her. "No."

Arthur gave him a superior look. "Raising horses is quite difficult, but my brother is an expert at it. What happened, didn't it work out for you?"

Caden's eyes burned into the man. "They

never made it back; they were murdered along the way and the horses stolen."

The room fell silent again. Caden watched Arthur's eyes flitting back and forth like he was trying to remember something. Then, they suddenly locked and widened.

Caden stood up from the table. "Thank you, Mrs. Stanford, for the supper, but I should be going."

Jo followed him out as he picked up his hat and stepped outside. "Oh Caden, I . . . I'm so sorry. He can be such a wretched person at times. I'm so embarrassed."

Caden took her hand. "Don't be, you're not responsible for his actions. I would like to call on you again . . . if you don't mind."

"You would? After that?"

Caden smiled. "I want to call on you, not your father."

"Oh, yes, I would like that."

The door opened behind them and Mrs. Stanford stepped out. "I want to apologize for my husband's behavior; he can be such a jackass sometimes, actually most of the time. He ran a dry-goods store in Mankato and now he thinks he's a westerner. He knows nothing about cattle, but tries to be the big man. He thinks that by acting like that, he's being tough."

"He won't make any friends out here like

that. He might even get himself shot if he keeps it up."

"Try telling him that. He thinks all he needs out here is that brother of his. Once again, I apologize."

Caden shrugged. "That's him, though. Why don't you and Jo come out to the house? I'm sure my ma would love to meet you, Mrs. Stanford. Ma spends most of her time with the ranch and ranch hands, I'm sure she would welcome a visit."

"Thank you, Caden, I'd like to meet someone my own age as well. My husband thinks I should be friends with his brother's wife," she gave an exaggerated shiver, "but I dislike the woman. Fortunately, I've only had to meet her once and that was quite enough thank you. She's unpleasant, to say the least."

Jo nodded. "Yes, I don't like them either, and father can't brag enough about his brother. It makes me ill."

Mrs. Stanford agreed and then looked back at Caden. "You see, Caden, Arthur told me that he and his brother left Missouri before the war. They separated and never saw each other again until we moved here. Arthur was living in Mankato when I met him; his brother had come here. It seems odd, though, that Arthur is suddenly so enamored with his older brother because he had never spoken of him prior to coming here." She laughed without humor. "A lot of things seem odd since we moved here."

"Yes, Mother, it is odd. It is almost as if we moved here strictly so he could be with his brother."

"Whom he never said much about until recently. I always assumed there was animosity between them."

Caden's curiosity was up. "If he moved here for his brother, wouldn't he have moved closer to him? Why this far away?"

"That too is odd, Caden. It all makes my head hurt trying to figure it out."

"You both should come out to the ranch for a break. Come sometime in the next couple of days and we'll all get better acquainted."

Jo looked at her mother. "Yes, we would like that wouldn't we, Mother?"

The older woman nodded. "Yes, get away from Arthur and his infernal bragging about Dillon."

Jo looked at Caden. "We don't know where you live, though, Cade. Come to think about it, I just realized that I don't even know your last name."

He smiled at her. "It's MacMahon."

Both women looked at him with startled

expressions. Jo asked, "Are you from the MacMahons who have the huge ranch up on the river and settled here when there were still Indians to fight? The man in the store mentioned your family."

Caden grinned. "My ma and pa, and Uncle Miles, came here in '55. I came along a bit later."

The women looked at each other and laughed. "Your father was bragging about this puny place to a MacMahon. Oh, that is funny."

"And arguing about everything and giving advice besides." Jo laughed lightly and shook her head.

She then turned serious. "Is it true that the outlaws are dangerous around here?"

Caden nodded. "Yes, it can be dangerous, so use caution when you are out. With so little law hereabouts, outlaws have an open field."

"Do you really hang them?"

"Yes."

"Do we need to worry about outlaws here?"

Caden shrugged. "Maybe. Yours is a small enough place they might pass you by; then again, they could see it as an easy steal. You could be wiped out overnight. But, if that happens, send word to me and we'll have half a dozen men here to deal with them and get your cattle back."

Jo paused in thought and then spoke to her mother. "Why did Father say he didn't know the Feldmans who raise the Morgan horses?"

"I don't know. They were regular customers at the store; we knew them well. It is odd, isn't it, that he would say that?"

"Everything is odd here, Mother."

CHAPTER FIVE

Three days after Caden's visit to the Stanford home, Mrs. Stanford and Jo drove a buggy up to the front of the MacMahon house. Ita stepped out on the porch and greeted them. "You must be Jo and Mrs. Stanford; Caden told me you'd be by."

Mrs. Stanford smiled. "Yes, Caden said we should come by; I hope it is all right."

"Of course, always happy to meet the new neighbors. Step on down and come in, got coffee on the stove."

Ita saw Bren coming out of the calf shed and called out him. "Bren, would you unhitch the buggy and take care of Mrs. Stanford's horse?"

Bren came directly to her. She gestured toward him. "This is my youngest son, Bren."

He smiled up at the two women, who recognized him. Jo smiled. "We have met, Mrs. MacMahon."

"Oh, you did." She gave Bren a stern look. "I hope he was behaving himself."

"Oh, yes, he and another man were teasing Cade for helping to load our wagon instead of theirs."

"Yeah, that would be Miles. Two peas in a pod, them two. Well, come on in."

The two women stepped out of the buggy with Bren assisting Mrs. Stanford. She smiled at him. "So, you *can* be a gentleman."

"Shh, don't tell anyone, it will ruin my reputation."

The women climbed the three steps up to the porch. Ita extended her hand. "We aren't much on formality around here, I'm Ita."

The women shook hands, with Mrs. Stanford saying simply, "Anna."

Ita looked at Jo. "Caden has told me about you."

"I hope it was favorable."

"He's smitten, and I can't say I blame him."

Jo blushed slightly, but smiled, pleased with the answer.

Ita led them into the kitchen and asked the women to sit around the table. Lifting a blue enamel coffee pot off the hot stove, she poured them each a cup. "I hope you don't mind sitting in the kitchen; I kind of prefer it to the other rooms."

Anna smiled. "Not at all. I was raised on a farm and my folks always sat around the kitchen table. It's only since I married and moved to town, with a town home, that we took to sitting in the parlor."

"Understand you folks are raising some cattle."

"In a small way. My husband's brother, who lives out here, wanted him to move down here from Minnesota and raise cattle. So, we did. They have been spending a good deal of time together since we arrived. In fact, he's off to his brother's now."

"Where is his brother at?"

"A town called Stanfordville. My understanding is that he built the town, or owns the businesses, or is somehow prominent there. It's named for him."

Ita shook her head. "Not familiar with that town. So, how do you like it here?"

"We love it, it is so beautiful."

"Yeah, we like it. Came here about twenty-five years ago, Owen and me. Miles, his brother, was with us. We've built the ranch up since then."

"You must have been the only ones around."

"There were a few others, mostly Indians,

though."

"It must have been dangerous."

Ita shrugged. "We had a fight or two with the Sioux until we all decided to get along. The Poncas were never a problem. How long has your husband's brother been out here?"

"I'm not sure. My husband, Arthur, said that they parted ways in Missouri before the war broke out. Dillon went on west and Arthur only as far as Mankato. Arthur had rarely mentioned his brother and never spoke of their lives before leaving Missouri. We never heard from Dillon until recently and then out of the blue he sends Arthur a letter telling him to move here and away we went."

"Kind of sudden, wasn't it?"

"Very. We had a store and were established in the community. One day he gets this letter; we sold the store and were off. He's been talking about his brother ever since."

"How do you like his brother?" Caden had already told her about the talk he had with them and how Arthur had acted.

Anna frowned, but didn't want to air the family's dirty laundry to a new friend, as she already had with Caden. "I've only met him once, so I really don't know much about him."

Their visit was interrupted by a loud bell clanging across the yard. Anna looked at Ita with a questioning expression.

"That's the noon meal bell. The boys in close will hit it like a charging bull; the rest will wander in for the next hour as their work allows them to. Give them a few minutes and then we can head up without getting stampeded over."

A quarter of an hour passed before Ita declared it was probably safe to head up to the cook shack. They left the house with Ita leading the way. The door was open to let in some breeze and release pent-up heat from the fired-up cook stove. They walked in and saw men sitting at the tables. Sam was behind a table that held plates of sliced meat and pots of steaming stew and beans. A pot of coffee and slices of bread on a plate completed the noon meal.

Sam looked up and smiled, his eyes stalled momentarily on Jo's face. "We have special guests, I see." He announced to the room, "We've got ladies in the room, boys, first one spits out a cuss word answers to me."

The men seated at the long tables looked at the women. They each stood and nodded an acknowledgment. Those still wearing their hats took them off. They stole admiring looks at the young woman.

Ita grinned at Sam. "We hired Sam out of a fancy hotel in Omaha. Seems he didn't kowtow to the *right* people and he got fired. He came to work for us and is the best cook in the country."

Sam smiled back at her. "I'd rather cook for cowboys who appreciate it than a bunch of rich snobs who complain because they don't have a decoration on their plate."

Bren and Miles were sitting at the family end of the table. The women followed Ita's example and filled their plates. They moved to the table and slid into the bench beside them.

Ita looked Bren and Miles over. "Don't need to call you two twice for grub, do we?" They grinned at her.

Miles nodded toward the Stanford women. "Ladies."

They smiled back at him with Anna commenting, "Mr. MacMahon, the man who doesn't want to spoil his reputation by working."

"That's me, ma'am."

Ita looked from Miles to Anna. "He'd like everyone to think that. Fact is, Miles can outwork any two men. He just believes that admitting it doesn't fit with his station in life."

A shuffling of boots was heard on the floor

coming into the shack. They turned to see Caden walking in with another man discussing cattle. Caden looked across the room to see Jo smiling at him. He smiled back at her and concluded his talk.

He walked up to the table. "Morning, Jo. Mrs. Stanford. I see you made it here all right."

Anna nodded toward him. "Nice to see you again, Caden."

Jo spoke excitedly, "We have been having a wonderful visit with your mother."

"Good. Let me fill a plate and I'll be right back." He moved toward the food table.

Caden turned toward the open door at the sound of a hard-ridden horse. He heard the horse slide to a stop, the slap of leather and metal tack, and a man's boots hitting the ground and running. He was angry that one of the men would approach the cook shack in such a way.

George Carson burst through the doorway, saw Caden, and shouted, "Randy's been shot!"

Caden left his plate on the table as all eyes turned toward George. Caden snapped, "What happened?"

George was trying to say it all fast. "Rustlers. We caught them with a bunch moving down through Rocky Draw. We yelled at them and they started shooting. They hit Randy and I got one of them. They put the bunch into a run and headed east."

"How bad is Randy?"

"Bad. He took a bad one. I got him to the line shack, tried to stop the bleeding, and headed straight here."

Ita moved quickly. "That's the same area we caught them other two last month." She took charge. "Caden, you, Bren, and Miles get out there and on that bunch right now." She pointed at a man standing beside the table. "Henry, get the wagon hitched up and bring Randy back here. George, head for town and get the doctor, there's one in Dukeville; it's closer."

George protested, "With all due respect, Mrs. MacMahon, they shot my partner."

"Right, sure, go with Caden." She pointed at another man. "Carl . . ."

Carl was up and moving. "On my way." He burst out the door, jumped on his horse, and was out of the yard at a gallop.

She looked at Sam. "Get your medical stuff and go with Henry." Sam cast off his apron and went into the back kitchen where he kept his supplies for patching up injured cowboys.

The shack was suddenly a flurry of activity with men moving in all directions.

Caden looked at Jo. "Sorry, Jo, can't stay."

Her face was drawn with worry. "I understand, go."

As quickly as the room had burst into activity it turned quiet. The sound of moving horses and the wagon being hitched emanated from the yard. Ita turned toward her guests. "Sorry to bust up your visit like that."

Anna shook her head. "No, you must take care of such a thing immediately. I say, though, I am impressed at how everyone responded to the emergency."

"We have a good crew here, more like a big family. Most of the boys have been with us for years and we take care of each other. Randy's been with us a long time, maybe ten years. George and Randy work out of our southeast line shack; they had rustlers down there last month, and now again. That's too much coincidence. We've had rustling problems off and on for years, but I'm thinking we have a gang working that part of the country."

"Cade told us," Jo began, "that there were outlaws around here and it could be dangerous."

"We do, and it can be. You have to keep your eyes open all the time."

"What will Cade and the others do when

they catch up to the men who took the cattle?"

Ita didn't hesitate with her answer. "The ones the boys don't shoot, they'll hang. Especially since they shot one of our own."

"Yes, Cade said you hang them."

Ita scrutinized the young woman. "Does that bother you?"

"No. At first when Cade said that, I admit, I was startled. In Minnesota that would never happen."

"This isn't Minnesota."

"Yes, I know, it is different here. I am coming to understand that. If you feel the need to deal harshly with thieves and murderers because there is no other way, I can accept that."

Ita looked at Anna for her reaction. Anna's face was stern. "I think all murderers and thieves should be hung."

Ita's expression revealed approval in the women's feelings. "I'm sure someday it won't be like that, but for right now it is necessary."

Ita cast a quick glance at Jo. "You'll do well here."

Slightly surprised by the comment Jo looked at her. She wondered if Ita meant, "you'll do well" in Nebraska or "you'll do well" *here* on the ranch. The idea of marrying Cade had danced in her mind, but they had only just met. However, Ita's comment made her wonder if she were already considered part of their family. The idea was not unpleasant to her.

The men reached the line shack an hour after George had ridden into the yard. They went inside to find Randy lying on his bunk. He was cold. George stood looking at him. On Randy's chest was a scribbled note. George grabbed at it, but Caden picked it up ahead of him.

George looked over Caden's arm to the note in his hand. It read simply, *My wages to my ma. George s . . .* The message ended with a pencil line dragging off the paper after the "s" as Randy died.

Caden looked at the note and figured Randy was trying to say "George saddle" when he died. Giving your saddle to your partner was a normal parting gesture. He folded the note and put it in his pocket. Randy sent part of his wages every month to his aged widowed mother in Cheyenne. Caden would make sure she got them.

He left a note for Henry and Sam telling them to take Randy's body back to the house and they'd return when they had caught his killers. They loaded their saddlebags with the food from the line shack. They changed to fresh horses from the corral and rode out on the trail left by the stolen cattle.

They rode down the draw where the shooting had started. They found the outlaw George had shot where his partners had left him. He was dead. Miles got down and pushed the body over on its back. He shook his head, "I've never seen him before. Any of you?" They all shook their heads.

Henry pulled the wagon up to the line shack. They saw the lathered horses in the corral and knew the men had already been there. They jumped down from the wagon with Sam carrying the infantry rucksack that held his medical supplies.

Henry pushed the door open and took a quick look around. He saw Randy lying under his blankets and knew at once that he was dead. He sagged a little, "Oh, hell." He and Randy had been good friends.

Sam picked up the note, read it, and handed it to Henry as he said, "Randy was a good man. I hope they find them."

Henry read the note. "Miles can track a bug across a stone floor; they'll find them. I only wish I was with them so I could pull on the rope."

Sam nodded in agreement. "Let's wrap

him in his blankets and take him back."

Sam pulled open Randy's blood-soaked shirt and took a quick look at the wound and shook his head. Together they worked with the body that had up until a few hours ago been one of their friends. They carried Randy, wrapped in his bloody blankets, as gently as if he were breakable. They laid him in the wagon bed and began the unhappy ride home.

The sound of the approaching wagon brought Ita out of the house. Anna and Jo followed. The first thing Ita saw was the drawn-down faces of Henry and Sam, then she looked to the stiff length of rolled blankets in the bed. The usual hard front that was the shell Ita MacMahon wore began to break. Her voice shook slightly. "Is that Randy?"

Both men nodded. Henry spoke with a low voice, "He was gone when we got there."

Sam added, "Cade and the others had changed horses and were gone."

The hands that were close in came to look at Randy. They shook their heads and muttered under their breaths. Ita understood and let them linger. She called out to one of the men, "Cletus, go catch Carl before he drags the doctor all the way down here. We won't need him anymore." The young cowboy nodded and strode toward his horse.

Randy was thirty-eight years old and had covered a good deal of country before hiring onto the OM. He had made his way up from Texas as a drover on the Goodnight-Loving Trail and eventually worked his way to Nebraska where he met Rafe. He had fought Comanches and Sioux and was a man wise in the ways of men. He was a friend of Rafe's and it was Rafe who had talked him into signing on.

Jo wiped tears from her eyes. She didn't know Randy, but the sadness in those at the ranch was testimony to his being a respected man and friend. That was enough for her; she felt what they felt.

Ita turned toward Anna and Jo, her voice soft. "What we were talking about before, yes, we do have our outlaws." She looked back toward the body in the wagon and her voice strengthened with anger. "And when we find them we kill them like the dogs they are."

Anna spoke to Jo, "We should go."

Ita shook her head. "No, you won't get home until after dark. I'm not sure what's going on, but it is better to be safe. We have an extra room; I want you to stay the night."

"I would feel better if we stayed, Mother."

Anna agreed. "Arthur will be a couple of days with his brother. We will stay."

Rafe rode into the yard looking curiously at the men gathered around the wagon. He had been in Niobrara and was unaware of what had taken place in his absence. He rode up to the wagon, his eyes asking the question as he looked at Henry still on the wagon seat.

Henry looked at Rafe. "It's Randy. Him and George ran into rustlers again."

"Oh, my Lord." Rafe's voice was subdued. "George?"

"He's okay; he's riding after them with Cade, Bren, and Miles."

Rafe stepped out of the saddle and put his hand on the blanket roll. He was stunned at the loss of his friend. He had assigned Randy to the line shack by his own request because Randy preferred it out in the hills.

He looked up at Ita standing on the porch. It was the first time since she realized Owen and Aiden were gone for good that he had seen her shaken. She looked back at him, a silent message of loss passed between them.

Abandoning his usual propriety of saying Mrs. MacMahon in front of the men he said, "Ita, this might only be the beginning. I was talking to a couple of ranchers I know from around the reservation. Seems there's been a rash of criminal activity down their way the last few months. Cattle rustled, a stage robbed, travelers robbed, and one or two murders. They're thinking a gang has moved into the area."

"That's what I was thinking, Rafe. That's twice we've been hit in that same corner of the ranch."

"I don't know if those two we caught last month were part of this gang or acting on their own accord. This gang seems to be bent on violence and what little anyone has seen of them, it looks like they work in large numbers, not like those two. One of the men I talked to said their tactics reminded him of the Reb Guerrillas and Jayhawkers from the war. If that's true, they will not hesitate to kill."

Ita's frown deepened. "If that's so, no one will be safe."

"That's what happened in states east of us. Especially in Kansas when the herds were coming through from Texas. We need to be armed from here on out, at least until this bunch is wiped out. If we encounter them, we will shoot to kill."

"Make sure the men all pack guns. I wonder if Major O'Connor knows."

Rafe shrugged. "I have no idea, but if he

102

does, maybe he can send some troopers to run them down."

"We'll have to make sure he's told. In the meantime, I want all the men not only armed, but working in pairs whenever possible."

"The men in the line shacks are taking turns riding night watch."

"I know. They can't both stay up twenty-fours a day and we need the night watch. Even if we sent up a third man, someone doesn't sleep." Ita frowned at the thought and sighed, "Tell them to be careful."

"I'll make sure everyone partners up who can." He looked at the blanket-wrapped body, took a deep breath, and let it out. His eyes reflected pain and loss. "We should bury Randy."

CHAPTER SIX

The trail of the stolen cattle and the riders that pushed them continued to the bottom of the cut that was known as Rocky Draw, named for the large rocks protruding out of the hillsides. There had been little rain, leaving the grass dry and the soil soft and dusty. The churned-up trail was easy to follow down through the draw.

Once out of the draw, the cattle tracks spread out. A set of shod horse tracks were found along each side of the herd. A rider on each side was keeping the animals bunched together. Two sets of horseshoe tracks were directly on top of the cattle's from the drag riders who pushed the cattle, keeping them moving. It was assumed that one man rode in front leading the herd. His tracks would be obliterated by those of the cattle. That made for at least five men. George thought he saw six; one was dead, leaving the five whose tracks were seen. That was not a firm number. There could be more and they could also pick up others along the way.

The killers had at least a two- to three-hour lead on them. Men riding hard could overtake men driving cattle even with such a head start. Matters could change, however, should they scatter in different directions. It would be impossible to catch them all. The trail continued into a wide expanse of grass, crossed it, and moved down another draw. At the bottom of the draw, the trail crossed a stream and continued east through a half mile of open country.

The MacMahon riders splashed across the stream and stopped at the edge of the grass looking over the open half mile to the next row of hills. They could see nothing of the cattle, but the trail was easily seen crossing the open area and funneling down into another draw. They moved on across the grass and down the draw.

Once on the east side of the stream, they were off the OM property. They were now on the neighboring ranch of Jason Young. It was one of the boundaries they hadn't fenced. Jason was a good friend and they shared this portion of range as well as lending hands back and forth at roundup.

At the bottom of the draw, the thieves

stopped and apparently waited for someone, evidenced by the meandering tracks of the grazing cattle. Miles circled the area, sorting out tracks. Three sets of shod horse tracks came from the east and met the herd. It seemed to be a predetermined rendezvous spot.

After several minutes Miles rode back to where the other men waited. "Okay, here's what we got. Three new riders picked up the cattle and continued on further east. The five we were trailing left the herd and headed north. We've got two choices; we can get the cattle back or run down Randy's killers. Which do you want to do?"

Caden scowled, he wanted both. He looked east and then he looked north and gritted his teeth. "Damn."

Bren shifted in his saddle. "We could split up, two go after the cattle, two after the men."

Miles shook his head. "I wouldn't recommend that. We're outnumbered as it is; we can do one or the other, but if we split our ranks, someone isn't coming back."

Caden agreed. "Miles is right. These men have shown they won't hesitate to kill. We need to stay together."

Miles watched his nephew struggle with the decision. "Cade, mind if I give you my

106

two cents' worth?"

"Please do."

"The cattle will likely be merged into a bigger herd and kept moving or hid in the hills. Around these parts you could lose half the Sioux nation in between a couple of hills, and that's no exaggeration, speaking from experience. We might never find them even if we searched until hell froze over. On the other hand, we can track those men and kill them, which will have the added benefit of keeping them from killing and rustling again."

Caden stared off to the hills. "If we can't recover the cattle, we can still show what happens when you steal MacMahon cattle and shoot our men. Is that what you're saying?"

"You got it."

"We can breed more cattle, but we can't bring back a good man once he's dead. We owe them for Randy." Caden kicked his horse to the north. "Let's kill some outlaws."

The trail left in the sandy soil by the rustlers was easy to follow. They were feeling confident that, with the cattle shunted off to their friends, they were in the clear. Any pursuit would be for the cattle, not them. Miles sorted out the tracks and meandering trails left by the men and confirmed that there were five of them.

They were following the trails when Bren looked across the open grass. "Riders coming."

They pulled up and watched the three men approach. As they drew closer, the three riders spread out in a defensive tactic. The MacMahons held their ground; Miles pulled his rifle from the scabbard and laid it across the pommel of his saddle. When they were close enough to recognize, Caden said, "It's Jason."

Miles pushed the rifle back into the scabbard. Jason Young rode up beside Caden and extended his hand. "Cade." He nodded toward the others. "Boys."

The two men with Young pulled in beside the group and exchanged greetings.

"What brings you out our way, Cade?"

"Running down rustlers. They killed one of our men this morning and made off with some cattle. We trailed them onto your place and then the cattle were herded east and the men we were trailing headed north."

One of Jason's men asked, "Who was killed, Cade?"

"Randy."

"We knew Randy, hell of a nice fellow."

Jason broke in. "So, they finally ranged

out your way, did they? We've had a bunch of thieving going on lately between here and the Missouri. My men and I have been riding a circuit around the ranch hoping to catch them at it. Sorry about Randy, he was a good man. I take it you've decided to hunt them down and leave the cattle."

"We couldn't do both. We decided it was more important to set an example and make them pay for killing Randy."

Jason nodded his understanding. "Might as well, once cattle are rustled, they're usually gone for good." He chuckled without humor. "Crossing a MacMahon is a death warrant. Guess these rustlers must be new around here not to know that."

"What can you tell us about this new thieving?"

"Unfortunately, not a whole lot. It's mostly been in the last couple of months. Oh, we've had a little here and there like always, but this is different; it's done with a direct purpose. It's not just a couple of drifters looking to sell a couple of head for drinking money. This is organized."

"Why do you think that?"

"Lots of cattle are being rustled, but there's more. A couple of stages have got held up along that road by the river. The passengers said it was a group of men wearing masks, flour sacks with eyeholes cut out. There's been a bunch of highway robberies and a couple of murders too. The marshal out of Yankton came down, but he's one man with a big country to law in. He can't sit around here waiting for these coyotes to try something."

"Has anyone recovered their stolen cattle?"

Jason shook his head. "Word has it that they get drove to the Burlington line where a man who doesn't notice brands buys them. He loads them on the cars and sends them east for top dollar."

Bren asked, "How about the Army? Are they doing anything about it?"

"They're just a token unit left here to make sure the Santee behave themselves. They don't patrol the country like they used to when the Indians were riding for scalps. They don't figure it's their problem, that it should be handled by the local law."

"There is no law up in this corner, local or otherwise."

Jason spit a stream of tobacco juice. "That's why it's up to us to deal with it."

"Coming from a former lawman," Miles put in, "I prefer it this way. No middleman to interfere. No sympathetic jury, no flannel-tongued lawyers, just justice dealt out straight and simple."

"You MacMahons have been here longer than I have, but as you recall, I came up with a herd from Texas in '67 and put down stakes. That's how we dealt with outlaws back there, shoot the ones you can and hang the rest. We didn't mess with 'em in Texas."

"Which is what we plan to do with this bunch when we catch up to them."

"Speaking of, we're holding you boys up from running down your killers. I'd offer to ride along, but you look like you got it handled."

Miles grinned at him. "We know how to skin a coyote."

Jason laughed. "Yeah, boy, that's a fact. Well, good hunting." The three men reined their horses around and rode back the way they had come.

Caden watched Jason Young and his men ride away. "I recall Pa saying that when Jason first rode into this country, he was a man tougher'n whale bone, and a good neighbor to have. That's always been the case too."

Miles agreed. "I knew his like in Texas. I wouldn't want him for an enemy. We've got some daylight left. Let's move on a bit more and then find a camp for the night. We can't track in the dark anyway."

The men continued riding north toward the southern end of the Santee reservation. Bren looked around him. "What are they going to do, ride right onto the reservation?"

Miles answered, "They better not. The Santee aren't happy about losing their hunting grounds to whites and getting shoved onto a little piece of hilly land. They're liable to kill any white man who doesn't have a purpose there, just for spite."

"Chances are," George put in, "they've kept right on going into Dakota and will disappear. We won't get a chance at them at all."

Caden glanced back at him. "I don't think you need to worry about that. They'll find a saloon to hole up in and get drunk. We need to follow until their trail ends at one."

George didn't say anymore, but frowned.

Just before twilight they came to where the outlaws' trail reached the southern border of the reservation and turned east. Camp was made for the night in a low area surrounded by trees where their fire wouldn't be seen from a distance. At first light they moved on.

The hot weather kept the ground dry and dusty. With the exception of some blown sand, the tracks hadn't changed since the day before. Caden studied the trail. "Miles, you get the feeling these men know exactly where they're going?"

"Noticed that, have you? Yeah, no meandering, they have a destination in mind, but I'm betting they found a settlement with a saloon and stayed the night in it. If they were drinking into the late hours, they'll be sleeping it off."

Bren laughed. "While we catch up."

It was noon when the distant sound of a hammer ringing off an anvil could be heard. The trail continued on toward the sound. Miles turned in the saddle to those behind him. "We might be coming up on something now."

Riding out from a draw, they came to a stretch of open land and several rough buildings along a narrow stream. A blacksmith shop, the source of the ringing hammer, was the first building they reached. The settlement was only a few buildings set in a straight line with a churned-up trail of dust serving as a street.

The blacksmith looked up at them as they rode by. He took a measure of the mounted men and knew they were on the hunt. Miles pulled up next to him. "You got a saloon in this town?"

With sweat glistening on his dirt-streaked

face, the man pointed with a big calloused hand. "Yonder, end of the row."

"Five men ride in here yesterday?"

"Can't say, a lot of men pass through here."

Miles gave him a hard glare. "Can't say or won't say? Never mind, we'll find out for ourselves."

They started to ride on when Caden pointed at five horses tied to three different railings in front of the end buildings. Miles held up and spoke over his shoulder to the blacksmith. "You got an undertaker in this town?"

"No."

"You got shovels?"

The blacksmith remained silent. Miles touched spurs to his horse. "Best get 'em out if you got 'em."

A wagon, hitched to a pair of stout horses, was in front of a store while a man loaded supplies. A second man, probably the store-keeper, stood next to him. The two men looked at them as they passed. Activity showed in the other buildings, but there were few people moving about on the street.

Pulling up to the far side of the rough board saloon, they dismounted. Leaving their horses ground tied, George and Bren stayed by the horses, keeping an eye on everything around them. Caden and Miles walked up to one of the tied horses.

Caden wiped his hand over the white dry powder covering the horse. All five had a dried coat of sweat salt over them. He looked at Miles and they exchanged a silent confirmation that they had the right horses.

Miles pointed at the piles of manure behind the horses. "These horses have been tied here for a spell."

"Since last night at least." He looked toward Bren and George and nodded. They walked up to Caden and Miles.

Miles pulled his Colt, flipped open the gate, and loaded a sixth brass cartridge into the empty chamber. He re-holstered the gun. The others did as well.

A farmer in a wagon drove past them continuing on to the store. He pulled in beside the first wagon, got down, and joined the two men standing in front of the store. The men watched the strangers and talked among themselves. The blacksmith's hammer had stopped and he was watching as well.

Being the most experienced with this type of situation, Miles took charge. "They might all be in there together. Chances are they're not, maybe two, maybe three are. The others could be anywhere; we don't want them getting us in a squeeze. Our advantage is they don't know we followed. They won't be set up for us."

Miles looked down the row toward the blacksmith's shop. The sun was at full strength, blasting heat down on them. A gust of wind blew across the dusty street stirring up a dust devil that spun away from the buildings. He could see men down the way they had come watching them. They knew something was about to break the quiet of their day.

Miles studied George for a moment. The man's expression reflected anger, which would be natural for a man whose partner had just been murdered. He knew George only as a hand on the ranch. His understanding was that he had signed on with the OM that spring for the gather and branding, and then stayed on. He was a good hand and had the look of a man who had been over the trail and lived to talk about it. "George, I don't know your history, and I'm not interested in it. I just want to know if you've ever been in a gunfight before."

George gave him a look. The cold deadliness in George's eyes was the same as he had seen in hardcase gunfighters in the wild lands. "That man in Rocky Draw isn't the first man I've killed. I intend to go in there with you."

The answer suited Miles; there was more to George Carson than they knew. "No one's going to argue that you should get first crack at your partner's killers. You and me are going in the saloon and confront whichever of that outfit's in there." He looked at Caden. "You and Bren watch out here, make sure no one comes in behind us."

Miles looked at the outlaws' horses. "You know, it's just wrong to keep horses tied without food and water. Why don't you boys strip that gear off and run them out of here."

Bren grinned. "That'll smoke them out or at the least put them on foot."

Miles nodded. "I'm thinking it will. Besides, they're not going to need them in a few minutes anyway. Before you do, give us five minutes in the saloon and then start cutting them loose." He looked at George. "Let's do it."

Miles and George walked in through the open doorway. The room was dimly lit and smelled of tobacco smoke and dust. A twenty-foot-long bar made from mill-dried planks was to their right. Three tables with chairs were in the center of the room. Three men sat at one table playing cards. Two more sat at another table talking together

117

with a bottle and glasses between them. Two men stood next to each other at the bar. The barkeep stood behind the bar looking bored. He turned his eyes to them as they entered.

Miles sized up the men in the room. The card players looked like farmers or settlers. The two with the bottle were obviously ranchers discussing cattle. The two at the bar were covered in trail dust, their unshaven faces and clothes that had been lived in forever, fit with men who had been traveling the back country. They both wore pistols on their belts.

Miles and George walked up to the bar. Miles held up two fingers indicating two whiskeys. The barkeep placed two glasses down and filled them from a bottle. Miles dropped a pair of quarters on the bar. He tossed down his drink and then turned his head to face the men six feet down the bar to his left.

He spoke in a loud voice, "You boys ride those salt-dried horses out front?"

The two men looked up and then at Miles. "You talking to us?"

"I'm sure as hell not talking to the bar."

The two men continued to stare at him. "What business is it to you what horses we ride?"

"Where's your other three pals?"

Both men stepped back from the bar, their expressions wary as they studied Miles. Their eyes grew wider as George stepped away from the bar and moved four feet to Miles' left. His hand was on his gun. The two men stared hard at George. "Hey, what's going on here?"

George looked coldly at the man. "You shouldn't have stopped off to get drunk. That was the wrong thing to do."

The outlaw held George's eyes as he spoke, "A man has a right to a drink when he's finished his work."

Miles broke in, "That's fine, providing your work isn't making off with MacMahon cattle and killing a man."

Both men shifted their eyes to Miles. "You're crazy, mister, we've been cowboying out east of here and we sure never killed nobody."

"Actually, you did." Mile's expression did not change.

"If you want to accuse us of something, you'd better have a lawman with you. We never stole no cattle or killed nobody."

"We don't need a lawman. We're going to take care of this right here and now."

The outlaw looked from Miles to George, his expression wary and questioning.

119

George's hard features never changed. The outlaw looked back at Miles. He waved his hand at him. "Aw, you're crazy." As his hand came down he grabbed his gun. Miles had seen the move before and expected it. His went for his gun, but George was already shooting. The man to the left gripped his stomach and fell to the floor. George then shot him in the head. Shifting his gun to the right George fired three fast shots into the second man.

The sound of running horses came from outside as Caden and Bren slapped the horses free. The barkeep rose slowly from behind the bar, peeking over the top. The men at the tables were watching from their places on the floor where they had dove to escape flying lead.

Miles stood with his gun in his hand and looked over at George. "Hell, George, you could have let me have one of them."

"Sorry." He flipped the gate open on his Colt and pushed out the spent brass, the empty shells making a series of loud thumps on the wooden floor. He reloaded and holstered the gun.

Miles pointed at George and then at himself. "You and me are going to talk later."

They walked out of the saloon into the

street in time to see two men running toward where the horses had been tied. They drew their guns and began firing at Caden and Bren, who returned the fire. The initial MacMahon shots put one of the outlaws down. The second fired as he was running away. Miles hurried to his horse and pulled the Winchester from the saddle scabbard. He shouldered the rifle and shot the outlaw as he ran. The outlaw stumbled and sprawled face down in the dirt.

A fifth man began running for the trees along the stream bank. Bren jumped into his saddle and rode after him. The man splashed across the stream with Bren's horse just behind him. The horse jumped the narrow waterway. He was a horse accustomed to working cattle and saw the running man as a target no different than a cow and stayed with his dodging running pattern.

Bren rode directly into the man, running him over as he fell. The man screamed. Bren jumped off the horse and up to the man. The outlaw scrambled to his feet and threw a punch that missed. Bren hit him twice in the face knocking him to the ground. Miles, Caden, and George caught up to them.

Bren grabbed one of the man's arms as Caden locked an iron grip on the other arm.

They jerked him to his feet. His lips were bleeding and there were scrapes on his face where Bren's horse had caught him a glancing blow with a hoof. Miles stood in front of him as the outlaw stared at him.

Miles was holding his hemp rope, opening the loop as he looked at the outlaw. "Are you part of this new outlaw gang?"

The man looked at him as he stood with his arms held firmly by Caden and Bren.

"Who do you work for? You don't look smart enough to plan these raids on your own. I'm thinking you're a pawn and nothing more. So, who calls the shots?"

"I don't know."

"You might want to use your last few minutes atoning for your misdeeds and tell us the truth and where to find your boss."

Miles dropped the loop over the man's head, tightened it, and tossed the remainder of the rope over a tree limb above them. He caught the end and pulled the rope snug against the man's neck. "You see, I'm not joking around."

The man's eyes bugged out and sweat began to pour down his face. "I don't know what you're talking about."

"Who's the man that pays you?"

"I was just in town here."

"Why did you run?"

"I was scared."

"Scared of what?"

"You were running around shooting every-one . . . I got scared and ran, that's all."

"You don't know who pays you, huh?" Miles pulled the rope some more, stretching the man's neck.

"I swear, mister, I swear to God." His voice was high pitched and strangled. "I didn't do anything."

"Do you know where he has his gang?"

"I don't know anything about a gang."

"You don't know much of anything do you. Do you know who we are?"

The man shook his head, and then cast a pleading look toward George, who stood expressionless and watched. "The name MacMahon mean anything to you?"

The man closed his eyes and whispered, "Oh, damn."

"You made a big mistake. Who shot the man on our place?"

The man opened his eyes, looking from one angry face to another, stopping on George's face. "I don't know, I wasn't there."

Caden turned his eyes on George. "Was this man one of them? He's wearing enough trail dust to have been riding drag."

George stared into the man's face. "I can't

say for sure. I couldn't swear to it."

With his neck stretched as far as it would go and his head forced to the side, the man stared down his bright-red face at George, his eyes wild with fear. He croaked out, "Please, help me." Several men from the town were watching them. Caden frowned. "Let him go."

Miles looked at him. "We hang rustlers, Cade."

"We have no proof that he was one of the rustlers. We didn't catch him in the act and George can't swear he was one of them."

"Sure he is, he's lying through his teeth."

"I know he is, but we hang him with an audience and the U.S. Marshal will be coming for us. It was a fair fight earlier, they shot first, but we string this one up and it won't be. Let him go."

Miles, still holding the rope, glanced at the townsfolk and then let loose the rope.

"Hell. You're right."

The man fell to the ground. He was trembling and breathing fast.

George bent down, jerked the rope off over his head, and growled directly in the man's face. "You're stupid. Now, get out of here and don't come back this way, ever. Do you understand that?"

The man nodded vigorously. "You won't

ever see me again."

"We'd better not."

The man rose to his feet, his legs visibly shaking. He stumbled into the woods without looking back. They watched him as he clumsily ran through the trees. Bren looked at George. "He sure got familiar with you in a hurry when he thought you were his last hope."

George continued to watch the way the man had run. "A drowning man will grab onto anything or anyone to keep from going under. He just happened to latch onto me."

Caden studied George for several seconds. "It's almost like he knew you."

George shrugged, but said nothing.

Something wasn't quite right. George saw their expressions. "Sorry, Cade, I couldn't say for sure about him."

Caden nodded, "Sure."

The men who had been watching them drifted away to join the others gathering around the bodies in the rough street.

Miles said, "Looks like we're back to knowing little except east seems to be the source of all this trouble. I haven't been through that part of the country in years and there wasn't much outside of the river business back then."

"East of here doesn't narrow it down a

whole lot," Caden added. "That's a lot of country, it could even mean across the Missouri."

"I don't think they're riding the ferry across the river to rob stages and steal cattle. Remember, Jason said he heard they were moving cattle out of here by train from this side. That has to keep it in Nebraska."

"Doesn't matter. We don't have the time to look. There's too much to be done at home. We accomplished what we came for; it's time to head back."

CHAPTER SEVEN

By the time Caden and the men returned to the ranch, Randy had been buried. Ita had placed an order to have a headstone carved to mark his final resting place on the ranch. It was a gesture appreciated by the men who had worked with and respected Randy as a friend and a man. It was understood that loyalty to the MacMahons was returned in kind.

The next night after supper several of the hands gathered around Rafe in the cook shack. He listened to them and nodded. Rising, he approached the MacMahons at their table. They stopped talking and looked up at him.

He laid a stack of bills and several coins down on the table in front of Ita. "The boys decided to buy Randy's gear so the money could be sent to his mother."

Ita sat in silence and looked past Rafe to the men standing behind him. "Thanks, men, that's mighty big of all of you. I'll put this in the mail to her, along with Randy's wages, tomorrow."

The next morning Ita approached Caden as he was sitting at his desk sorting through ranch accounts. He stopped, leaned back in his chair, and looked up at her.

"You didn't get much of chance to visit with Jo the other day."

"No, I didn't. Matters were kind of wild that day."

"Her and Anna are good people. They stayed the night, didn't want them traveling alone in the dark not knowing what kind of danger was out there."

Caden smiled. "That was good thinking. So, you like her?"

"I like them both. Jo asked questions about you."

"I hope you said good things about me."

"I told her you were smitten with her."

Caden jumped forward in his chair and almost shouted, "You told her what?"

"You heard me. You are, aren't you?"

"Well, yes, but I don't think you should have said that to her. For Pete's sake, Ma, I just met the girl."

"Oh, stop your belly aching. She's smitten with you too."

128

Caden stared at his mother. "She is? How do you know? Did she say so?"

"I know, that's all. Women know these things. I fell in love with your father the minute I laid eyes on him. Do you know how we got married?"

"Said, 'I do' You may now kiss the bride, and all that?"

"Don't get smart. Owen and I got off that accursed ship in Boston Harbor. We went to the first church we saw and told the priest we wanted to get married. He didn't want to marry us because we were too poor, and immigrants, and a load of other blarney. Fact is, he wanted a nice tidy sum for marrying couples. We couldn't meet his price.

"Owen told him he could marry us or not, it didn't matter to him. If he refused, we'd live together in sin. The priest said we'd go to hell if we did. Owen told him, no, *he* would be the one going to hell for refusing to marry us and forcing us to live in sin. That did it, he gave us a quick ceremony. He didn't like it, and he didn't get paid, but he got to keep his soul.

"The point is, Caden, we knew we were right for each other from the moment we met and nothing was going to stop us. You and Jo are right for each other; she knows it and so do you and you had better not lose her by being timid."

"Maybe I should go see her right now."

"My thoughts exactly." She handed him a sealed letter. "This is to Randy's mother. Can you mail it before you ride out to see Jo?" She turned and walked away.

Caden walked in the door of the Niobrara post office and was greeted cheerfully by Abe Everts, the postmaster, who was behind the counter filling mail slots. Caden handed him the letter to Randy's mother and paid the proper postage for its delivery. Abe dropped it in the mail sack due to go out on the next stage-run west.

Abe turned from the mail sack back to Caden. "Word came up the road that you and your crew had a run-in with some outlaws."

"We did that all right. Six of them made off with a bunch of our cattle and killed one of our men."

Abe looked toward the mail bag. "Yes, Randy, we heard. He was a decent man."

Caden's face turned grim. "They won't be killing anyone again."

"I'm sure they won't be. Say, what do you hear about this outlaw gang that's rampaging around here? Those you had at, were they part of that gang?"

"They were. We've heard several times that the worst of it is east of us. Have you seen anything out of the normal around here? New faces maybe, that don't look like settlers?"

Abe thought silently for several seconds. "Neil said there was a pair in his place this morning that were new to him. He said they didn't look like cowboys, but they claimed to be new hands out at the Stanford place."

The name shocked Caden. "The Stanford place? He doesn't have enough work on that place to need a hired hand let alone two."

Abe shrugged. "I wouldn't know about that. That was the Stanford girl who took that fall last week, I hope she wasn't hurt."

Caden was busy wondering why Arthur Stanford would have two hands working for him. He answered absently, "No, she was fine. I think I'll ask Neil about those two men." He said good-bye and headed back out to the street.

He walked down to Neil's store. He was alone and greeted Caden as he stepped inside.

"How are you today, Neil?"

"Good. You look like you're visiting rather than buying."

"I was just talking to Abe; he said that you had a couple of strangers in here this morning. New hands out at the Stanford place?"

"Well, they claimed to be ranch hands, but they weren't. I worked in Abilene back when it was the end of the Texas trail drives. I seen a lot of cowboys, and trust me these men aren't cowboys. More like a couple of coyotes."

"Or outlaws?"

Neil nodded. "Or outlaws."

"Yeah, I was worried about that."

"Heard about the trouble at your place. Too bad about Randy. You think these two are part of that outlaw gang?"

"There's been a lot of unusual happenings around here lately. If there are outlaws working out at the Stanford place, I'd be worried for the Stanford women."

"What about Mr. Stanford, shouldn't he be watching out for his women?"

Caden frowned at the thought of Arthur Stanford. "I'm not so sure about him."

"I know what you mean. He came in here once. Thinks he's some big shakes as a cattleman. You ever notice how he says 'cattles'? I like to of burst out laughing when he said that."

"I think I'll ride out there and check on them." Caden bid goodbye to Neil and left the store.

He was concerned and confused. Why would Arthur need hands who weren't hands, and why did they look like outlaws to Neil? There was something not adding up in regards to Arthur Stanford. He put his personal feelings of dislike for the man aside and looked at the picture objectively.

Arthur bragged constantly about his older brother, Dillon, whom he had never mentioned, according to Anna, for twenty years. Then, out of the blue he gets a letter from Dillon, and on the strength of that letter from the brother who he supposedly hadn't seen in years and never talked about, he sells his store and uproots his family to move. Now he spends all of his time, to the neglect of his family and ranch, with this brother who happens to live to the east where all the trouble seems to be emanating from. It was strange.

It was possible he was spending time with his brother because they had not seen each other in years. He could also be learning the cattle business from him. So there could be legitimate reasons for the time spent with his brother. Maybe his brother *had* sent over a couple of hands to help him out. If that were so, why did they not look like hands? They looked like *outlaws*.

Jo said they had been on their place for

three months. In all that time they had only seen this Dillon and his wife once. Dillon never came over to their place. It was always Arthur going to him, in a town called Stanfordville, a place he had never heard of. It was also odd that the Stanford women had never been to Niobrara in those three months. It was the closest town of any size. It wasn't a long or dangerous trip. The questions hung disturbingly in his mind.

Mulling over the tangle of questions, he realized with a start that the outlaw gang had sprung up about three months ago. Up at the ranch they had only heard the stories recently, but Jason said that out his way it had been going on for a couple of months. That was about the same time the Stanfords had moved here.

He was arriving at the uncomfortable feeling that Arthur was involved with the outlaw activity. He was an irritating man, filled with himself, and ignorant of western customs, but he seemed too weak to be involved with an outlaw gang. Then again, if he was running the gang in the shadow of his tougher brother, he wouldn't need to be tough himself. There had to be a tie-in with Arthur, his brother, and the gang. It fit too neatly together.

So, where did that leave Jo? Was she part

of the operation? He shook off the idea; he didn't want to believe that she could be anything other than the sweet girl that he thought she was. He thought hard about the reactions Jo and her mother had to Arthur's behavior the night he was there. They genuinely were appalled. They had also indicated that he was often "wretched," as Jo put it, and a "jackass," as Mrs. Stanford put it. He concluded that Arthur's behavior was not unusual, but had intensified, since moving here. That reaction from the women would indicate that they were not involved. If they weren't involved, and Arthur was doing this without their knowledge, they were in danger.

Caden was brought out of his deep thoughts by the clattering of wood and chains, accompanied by the pounding of horses' hooves. He looked up to see the stage coming in fast and hard. The driver was shouting to everyone on the street to get the doctor. As the stage passed, he could see the shotgun guard lying on top of the stage between the boxes and bags.

The driver drove through town to the front of the doctor's office where he hauled back on the reins while pushing his foot down on the brake lever. The team came to an abrupt halt with the locked wheels sliding in the dust. The doctor rushed out of his office and climbed up on the stage. After a quick look at the shotgun guard, he shook his head and said to the driver, "This man is dead."

The driver pointed down to the coach while shouting to the growing crowd, "We got a wounded passenger inside."

The door was yanked open and a wounded man, groaning in pain, was pulled from the seats and carried to the doctor's office. A second man worked his way out of the coach looking dazed, yet uninjured.

The doctor climbed down from the coach and looked at the second passenger. "Are you all right?"

The man nodded. "Only frightened."

The doctor turned and followed the men inside, closing the office door behind him. The men on the street began to throw questions at the driver.

He explained that they had been hit by a gang of outlaws halfway between there and St. Helena. There were four of them and they wore sacks with eyeholes over their heads. The shotgun guard had gotten off one shot before he was hit.

The stage was forced to stop and the passengers ordered out and robbed. The one wounded passenger had refused to hand over his valuables and was shot. While he lay on the ground, one of the outlaws took his wallet and watch. They took a bank bag of money and rode off. The driver said they were cold blooded and ruthless, shooting without hesitation.

Caden listened with interest. There it was again, the same area where the other crimes had been committed. Only this time they had moved further to the north. The gang was ranging out into new areas. The questions about Arthur Stanford rose up in his mind again. Maybe it was all coincidence and the Stanford brothers had nothing to do with any of the outlaw activity; however, it was getting harder by the hour to accept that. He wanted to ask some pointed questions and hoped Jo and her mother could give him the answers.

He mounted and rode west back out of town. Turning down the road that followed Verdigris Creek, he rode until he came to the Stanford property. Not wishing to draw attention to himself by crossing the bridge, he moved the horse into the stream, crossing downstream from the house. He rode up a hill that overlooked the back of the house and the land surrounding it. Remaining on horseback he studied the scene before him.

Smoke flowed out of the stovepipe that protruded from the roof of the house. The two horses he had seen pulling the Stanford women's wagon and buggy were standing in a corral. The double doors to the barn that held the wagon and buggy were closed. He saw no movement and wondered where the two men were who were posing as the new hands.

He had been watching for only a few minutes when the back door to the house opened and Anna Stanford came out. She appeared to be nervous, looking from side to side as she quickly made her way to the root cellar that was dug into the base of the hillside behind the house. She lifted the heavy wooden door and disappeared. She reappeared carrying a jar in each hand. Setting the jars on the ground, she closed the door, picked up the jars, and repeated her nervous fast walk back to the house. She went in the house, closing the door behind her.

Caden couldn't help but wonder why the woman was acting so strangely. She hadn't struck him as the nervous or fearful type. It was time for some answers. He rode down the hill to the back of the house. He stepped out of the saddle and knocked on the door.

He waited a full minute with no one

answering the door. He knocked again and heard light footsteps approaching the door from the inside. The door opened slowly with only a few inches of opening between the door and the frame. He could make out Anna's face in the crack looking out at him.

"Mrs. Stanford, it's Cade MacMahon."

The door opened fully. "Quick, come in." She grabbed his arm and pulled him into the kitchen.

"Mrs. Stanford, what is going on around here?"

Jo came into the kitchen; her face was strained. He looked at her. "Jo?"

Jo began, "We don't know what is going on here anymore. Father is gone for days at a time. He says he is with his brother. And now, these men."

"The men? The two men your father hired?"

"How did you know about them?"

"Neil, at the store, told me. He said you had two new hands out here and they didn't look like ranch hands."

Anna shook her head. "Arthur did not hire them. He said his brother loaned him two of his hands to help with the ranch, but . . ."

"But, you don't believe that."

Anna shook her head. "No, I don't. They are never out working on the ranch. They come and go constantly, unless Arthur is gone, and then they stay around watching us. It gives me the shivers the way they look at Josephine, like starving dogs in a meat market. I am fearful for her and for myself."

Caden looked out the kitchen door toward the parlor. "Is your husband here now?"

Anna shook her head. "He is off again."

"Stanfordville?"

She snapped bitterly, "Where else!"

"Where is Stanfordville anyway?"

Anna shrugged. "I have no idea. The one time we met Dillon and his wife, Maude, it was here when we first moved in. It was an unpleasant visit. We have never been asked to Stanfordville or taken there. That suits me, though, as I could not last long in that woman's company without slapping her."

"That is strange, all right."

"At first Arthur wanted me to be friends with them; however, when I showed reluctance, he chose to keep me away from them."

"Mrs. Stanford, I have to ask you this, please don't take offense. The outlaw activity started about the same time you moved here. Is there any chance Arthur is involved with that?"

"I don't know what to think. If he is involved in something illegal with them, he knew I would not approve and that is why he has kept me away from them. I would hope not, but Arthur is a man I no longer know. So, yes, it is possible."

"He has never talked of his life before Mankato?"

Anna shook her head. "No. Only that he came from Missouri and he had a brother named Dillon who left there as well. I always thought they hated each other because he never spoke of him."

"Maybe he was hiding something."

"So much has happened that is strange, that I would not be surprised if he was."

Caden considered that for a moment before remembering the two men. "Are those men here now?"

"I don't know. We haven't seen them, but I think they are about somewhere."

"How does your husband act around these men? Does he appear to be afraid of them?"

"Quite the contrary, he seems to know them well."

Jo broke in, "As strange as it seems, they actually seem to be afraid of *him.*"

Caden thought silently for a second and then looked at Jo and then her mother. "You need to get out of here."

Jo shook her head. "We can't. When father is here he demands that we stay home. He brings supplies from Stanfordville so we don't need to go to Niobrara. When he is gone, we are too afraid of the men to leave the house."

"We are afraid to leave the safety of the house." Anna sighed almost in pain. "If they catch Jo out in the open or on the road, it could be terrifying."

Anger was building up in Caden. He disliked Arthur Stanford to begin with and this was unacceptable. That a man would put his wife and daughter in such peril and control their movements so completely was too much for him.

His suspicions that Arthur was involved with the outlaws were beginning to sound believable. However, there was still a chance he was merely as ignorant as he appeared, that his brother had actually lent him some men and he had no idea what kind of men they were. Still, he no longer believed that Arthur Stanford was that ignorant.

"If these men are around, where can I find them?"

"They have been living in a small room in the barn," Anna answered. "But, please, don't confront them, they are dangerous."

Caden scowled. "So am I." He went out the back door.

He walked toward the barn and found a

single door on the side. He entered the barn and looked around. The buggy and wagon were inside along with harness, tack, and tools hanging from the walls. Sunlight shone in through the cracks in the walls reflecting off the dust moving through the still hot air. In the far corner of the barn he could hear men's voices. He walked toward them.

He recognized the slur of drunken talk. The two were in the room drinking, which served to confirm that they were not ranch hands. He listened outside the room.

He went with his gut feeling that the two men were outlaws and likely part of the gang. These were men of low degree who caused the women to feel unsafe in their own home. Sober they might be forced to practice restraint, but drunk, they could be capable of anything. He remembered his father saying that a sober man's thoughts were a drunken man's words. That included actions. What a sober man might wish to do but doesn't, he will do when he is drunk.

He opened the door to the room. The two men sat on their bunks passing a bottle between them. They had enough liquor in them to be dangerous, but not enough to be incapable of fighting. They looked up at him as the man to his right growled, "Who are you?"

Caden glared him. "I'm the man that's here to kick you off this place."

The men looked at each other and laughed. The one on the right snorted. "The hell you say?"

"Pack up your trash and head back to your gang."

"We answer to Stanford, not you."

"Which one, Arthur or Dillon?"

The man on the left stared at him. "Hey, you must be that MacMahon fellow what's sweet on the girl. We was told to keep you off the place."

"You were huh, by who?"

The men squinted their eyes at him and swayed slightly in their drunken condition. "By Stanford, that's who."

Caden reached down and grabbed the man on the right by the front of his shirt and jerked him off the bunk. He threw him out the open room door, causing him to land face first in the hard packed dirt of the barn floor. Caden repeated the move with the second man. They both lay on the dirt floor cursing at him.

The first man lurched to his feet and charged, throwing a punch that missed. Caden slammed his right fist into the man's mid-section. A woof of air escaped as he fell to his knees. The second man came up swinging and received a fist in the face that sent him sprawling.

With a curse, the first man grabbed a shovel and began swinging it. Backing up, Caden pulled a bit and bridle off the wall, swung it like a sling, and slapped the bit hard across the man's face, causing a scream of pain. He dropped the shovel and grabbed his face, which was bleeding from several cuts.

Cade grabbed the man by the back of the collar and seat of his pants and ran him through the single door of the barn. He landed on his stomach and face, where he stayed moaning on the ground. Caden turned around and went back for the second man.

As Caden walked across the floor the man came at him with a hay fork. Caden pulled his Colt, thumbed back the hammer, and leveled it at him. "One more step and I'll kill you where you stand. Drop the fork."

The man dropped the fork and put his hands in the air. Caden gestured with the gun barrel toward the open door. "Get your pal and get out. Ride south and keep riding, don't ever come back here again."

"We'll go, but you played hell, Mac-Mahon."

"No, you played hell when you stepped

on MacMahon toes. Now, get out before I blow a hole in your belly."

The man hurried out of the barn, keeping his hands in the air and watching Caden. Their horses were saddled on the opposite side of the barn. Caden followed him as the outlaw untied the horses and led them back to where his partner still lay on the ground. He helped his partner into the saddle and then mounted. "We got our outfits and guns in the room, can I get 'em?"

"No, get new outfits. Now ride."

"You'll pay for this."

"Yeah, now you got me scared." He pointed at the stream. "South is that way, don't stop until you reach Kansas."

The men rode over the bridge and down the road. Caden watched them until they were out of sight. He returned to the house, going in the front door. The women were watching through the windows and turned when he entered.

"Those two told me that Stanford wanted them to keep me away from here."

Putting her hand over her mouth, Jo whispered, "I was afraid of that."

"We need to get you both out of here."

Jo agreed. "Mother, we must leave. There is something very frightening about father and his new friends."

Anna nodded. "Yes, we must, but where?"

"Our place." Caden answered her question.

The sound of a horse walking over the wooden bridge could be heard. They looked at each other, thinking the two men had returned. Caden looked out the window to see Stanford riding up to the house. "It's Arthur."

Jo groaned. "He'll never let us go."

"Not right now," Anna said, "but we will watch for our chance."

Caden stepped out on the porch and watched Arthur ride up to the house. His horse appeared to be favoring its right front quarter. His expression upon seeing Caden was one of unpleasant surprise. It was obvious he did not like Caden at his house; however, as he drew nearer he managed a false smile

"Hello, Caden, what brings you out this way?"

"I came to see Jo."

"Good, good, glad you came by."

Caden studied the horse; he was wet from running and the foam over the sweat indicated hard running. The horse was still catching his breath as white froth formed between the bit and his mouth. This horse had been run hard and far, but slowed down before reaching home so it would appear as if he had just casually ridden in. A man who didn't know horses might not recognize the signs.

As Arthur dismounted, Caden said, "I just ran your new hands off."

Arthur looked startled. "My brother lent them to me to help with the ranch. Whatever happened?"

"They were drunk and frightening the women. When I talked to them, they started a fight. I sent them packing."

That Arthur was upset and didn't appreciate Caden's actions toward the men was clear. It was an effort, but he held his feelings in check. "Oh, most certainly, you did the right thing. I can't have my wife and daughter threatened by brigands while I am away, can I?"

Caden thought, *brigands*? Brigands was a term not used in the west. It was a southern term he had heard used by some Kentuckians he had once met. They had used the word, brigands, in reference to a story they were telling him about outlaws on the Natchez Trace. It seemed an odd word for a man from Minnesota to use.

Caden looked at the horse's front shoulder and saw bleeding cuts. "Looks like your horse has been injured. He's bleeding on

148

his shoulder."

Arthur jerked in response to the comment. "Oh . . . yes. He ran into a barbed-wire fence on my way back from Stanfordville. I was about to treat it."

Caden wondered if the horse's cuts were from barbed wire or shotgun pellets. "So, where exactly is Stanfordville, Mr. Stanford?"

He pointed to the east. "About three hours ride that way."

"Did you hear that a stage was robbed out that way around noon? It must be part of that outlaw gang that's been working in that area."

Arthur shifted uncomfortably from one foot to the other. "Robbed? How awful." He made no comment in regards to the gang or to inquire as to the condition of the people on the stage.

"With as much time as you spend over in that country, you should be careful."

The implication in Caden's remark was not lost to Arthur. He glared at him and then smiled. "I have yet to encounter any problems."

"I'm sure you haven't." Caden watched the man to read his reaction and saw two things in Arthur Stanford's eyes, hatred, and to his surprise, fear. "I was just leaving.

149

Good day, Mr. Stanford."

"Good day, Caden." Arthur watched him as he walked away.

Caden walked around the house to the back where his horse was standing. He mounted and rode away and across the bridge. He was worried about Jo and her mother. He looked back to see Arthur still watching him leave.

It was late afternoon when Caden left the Stanford house and rode out onto the Verdigris Creek road. Riding deep in thought, he didn't notice the shadows growing longer into evening. By the time he reached the main road that led back to the ranch, twilight had set in. He turned to the west, putting Niobrara to his back. He looked up to watch a nighthawk while his mind was filled with thoughts of Jo and her safety.

As he bent over in the saddle to pull out a long weed that had got caught in the stirrup leather he felt something hit him hard in the back. The pain was unlike anything he had ever felt. He gasped for breath and felt himself falling. Something was wrong: his back was wet, he felt cold, and he couldn't stop himself from falling off the horse. Then, there was nothing.

CHAPTER EIGHT

It was a full-moon night, the air still warm from the heat of the day. Crickets made the silent night ring with the steady drone of their sound as two men met under the cover of darkness. One rode in from the north, the other from the west.

The man from the west jerked his head toward a grove of trees. "Under the trees; I don't like being lit up out here like a Christmas candle."

They moved their horses into the protection and shadow of the trees. The north man spit out angrily, "What the hell happened with Harley's men? Your little brother came back like a hysterical woman carrying on about everyone being killed and he was almost hung."

"Don't get tough with me. I've never been afraid of you, so watch yourself." Even in the dark shadows he could see the other man stiffen in his saddle.

The west man continued, "Those two you sent last month got themselves hung when they stopped to take a nap, and the fools were still on MacMahon property. Now, you recruit this last bunch. Don't seem like you're capable of hiring anything but idiots."

"What do you mean *I* recruited, you knew Harley as well as I did."

"Yeah, *you* recruited. I would never have trusted Harley to raid the MacMahons; he's got the sense of a two year old. You sent them in." He thought for a second, "You never told them it was MacMahons, did you?"

"They didn't need to know that. Besides, Ed was with them, he was supposed to stick to the plan."

"Well, they didn't. You don't stir up a hornet's nest like the MacMahons and then skip down the trail like little girls picking flowers. I've put in a lot of time scouting this thing out and we can pick off hundreds of head of MacMahon cattle if we do it right. *Right* is the key here, and it's not getting done *right* with the morons you're hiring, like Harley."

The north man took a deep breath and calmed his angry voice. The other man had always been quick to kill and he didn't want to end up on the business end of his gun.

"Tell me what happened."

"They stopped off to get drunk. What else would you expect from Harley?" He heard the other man sigh disgustedly.

The west man went on, "The orders were to run off the cattle *quickly* not lollygag about it. They took their sweet time about it. You can't do that with MacMahons. You have to hit them hard and fast and keep moving. The idiots lost a man right off."

"What do you mean, lost a man?"

"I mean while they was lollygagging, he got blown out of the saddle by a Mac-Mahon hand."

The man stared hard at the west man. "Did this hand recognize *anyone* that we know?"

The question was pointed at him and he didn't like it. "He's dead."

"That's good."

"Don't change the subject. We were talking about your blunder in hiring incompetent drunks. That was *your* mistake, don't try and shift the blame of the mess on me or Ed. Bottom line is they didn't follow orders and they're dead for it. Let it be a lesson to anyone else who can't follow orders."

The north man shook his head. "The instructions were simple."

153

"I guess not *simple* enough."

"They were supposed to drop the cattle at the pickup point and keep riding for Dakota without stopping. They were to lay low for a month before returning. They understood that. Hell, I gave them enough money to stay drunk the whole time."

"Well, they couldn't wait for Dakota to get drunk. They stopped at the first saloon they came to after dropping the cattle. That's where the MacMahons caught up to them."

"Okay, it was a mistake."

"Your mistake."

"All right, I got it, *my* mistake. Now, shut up about it. I think we should halt operations until things settle down. People are getting suspicious and starting to figure things out."

"People like who?"

He ignored the question. "We have been moving a lot of cattle and hitting stages. There's bound to be a posse or at least search parties out looking for us. If we shut down for a while, and let the dust settle, we can resume again once everything has calmed down."

The west man nodded. "I'll agree with that. With those idiots stirring up the Mac-Mahons, we had better. You don't know that outfit, you're new here, but you step on a MacMahon and they won't ever let up on you. Those people could gut this operation wide open."

"They're not as tough as they think they are."

The west man glared at him, the whites of his eyes eerie in the darkness. "You'd better damn well believe they are that tough. You don't mess with that outfit and walk away. Pass the word on to Dillon that we're laying low and tell him to do the same."

"I'll get word to him."

"I'll contact you next, don't look for me." He pointed his finger at the north man, "And keep your mouth shut, you always did talk too much, and don't do *anything* to rile up the MacMahons. One more incident with them and we'll be the ones gutted."

The west man turned his horse and disappeared in the darkness. The north man sat still on his horse and felt a sharp pain in his stomach. It was almost like a knife, like he was being gutted by a riled-up Mac-Mahon. He had made another mistake, a big mistake.

Ita knocked on the door to Miles' room. She heard bed springs squeaking, and then a shuffling of feet on the wood floor and movement. The door opened and Miles looked at her sleepy eyed. "Ita. What's up?"

"It's after midnight and Caden's not back yet, I'm getting worried."

Miles turned and grabbed his watch off the nightstand that stood between the door and his bed. Snapping it open, the hands confirmed what Ita had said. "He went to see Jo, didn't he?"

"Yes, fifteen hours ago. He should have been back long before this. I've got a bad feeling, Miles, a bad feeling."

Miles was wide awake now. "Yeah, he should have been back by now. I'll get Bren and we'll ride out and look for him." He didn't need to tell her that it was a dangerous time for one man to be out alone.

"Thanks, Miles."

He nodded and closed the door. Dressing quickly he buckled on his Colt and picked up his rifle from the corner of the room where it stood. Walking down to the next door he opened it and went in. Bren was lying on his back sleeping.

Miles shoved him hard. "Wake up."

Bren's eyes snapped open. "What?"

"Get your tail out of bed. We have to go look for Cade."

"He went to see Jo."

"Yeah, and it's after midnight and he's

156

still not back."

Bren grinned. "Maybe . . ."

"Don't say it. Your ma would wash your mouth out with soap for even thinking it. Come on, Sunshine, let's go. I'll be saddling up." He left the room, leaving Bren to rouse himself out of bed and sound sleep.

Miles had two horses tied outside the tack shed and was pulling the cinch on his saddle when Bren strode up to him. The bright full moon shone like a room lit by a lamp. The horses and corral posts cast shadows across the ground.

Bren leaned his rifle against the corral rail and ducked inside the tack shed. He returned carrying his gear. Tossing a saddle blanket over the horse's back he dropped the saddle in place. After tightening the cinch, he slid the bit into the horse's mouth and set the headstall. Pushing his rifle into the scabbard he glanced up at the moon. "It's a good night for looking."

Miles pulled the reins loose and mounted. "I hope it's a good night for finding."

Caden had told them that the Stanfords lived on the Verdigris Creek road. Verdigris Creek branched off the main road a half mile west of Niobrara and followed the creek south. They knew the road. They also knew that Caden would stick to the established roads when riding in the dark. If he was on the road, they would find him.

They rode along in silence for the first half hour; the only sound being the footfalls of the horses and creaking of saddle leather. Bren broke the silence. "I hope he's all right."

"I hope so too."

"Because, if he is, I'm going to kill him."

Miles chuckled. "Brotherly love?"

"Younger brother deprived of sleep because older brother is playing Romeo and doesn't have enough sense to come home and not worry everyone to death. So, if he says, 'Oh, I lost track of the time,' I'll kill him."

"If that's the case I might help you. Actually, I hope that is the case. I agree with your mother, I have a bad feeling about this."

They rode on for another hour. The moon was lower to the horizon when Miles pulled to a stop. He peered into the night ahead of him. "Is that a horse standing in the road up there?"

"All our horses ground tie." Bren stared up the road. "It is a horse and he looks to be ground tied."

They moved on toward the standing horse. The horse lifted his head, recognizing his herd mates, and whinnied at them. Bren caught up the trailing reins and ran his hand over the saddle seat. He felt a sticky, dry substance on the seat; he held his hand up so the moon cast some light on it. His hand had a dark stain on it. "I think this is blood."

Miles glanced at his hand and rode past the riderless horse. He shouted, "Here he is."

Miles jumped off his horse and knelt over Caden. Bren was a second behind him. Miles dug a match out of his pocket and stuck it up. Holding the flame closer to Caden he could see the blood on him. He placed his hand over his heart and then put his ear on Caden's mouth. "He's still alive. Get into town and roust that doctor out of bed and come back with a wagon."

Bren jumped into the saddle and hit a gallop for Niobrara a half mile down the road. Miles examined Caden as best he could without moving him. He had been shot in the back and had lost a lot of blood. He hunkered in the road listening to the pounding of Bren's horse. He stripped Caden's gun belt off and rolled the belt around the holstered gun. "Damn back shooter," he mumbled.

Bren slid his horse to a dusty slide in front of the doctor's house, which also served as his office. Leaping from the saddle he ran up and began pounding on the door.

A man's voice from inside shouted not to break the door down. The door swung open and the doctor glared out. He spoke with a German accent. "Do you know what time this is?"

"I'm Bren MacMahon. Doctor, come on, my brother's been shot and he's in bad shape."

The sleep left the doctor's eyes. "Oh, yes, MacMahon."

"Yes, sir, hurry, Cade's been shot. He's laying in the road just out of town."

Realization came to the doctor. "Oh, Lord. I'll be right with you. Hitch up my rig, there's room in the back to carry a prone man."

The doctor went back inside and woke up his wife, who assisted him as a nurse. "Caden MacMahon has been shot and is lying in the road. I'm going with his brother to bring him in. Get the room ready."

As he hurriedly dressed, his wife jumped out of bed. "What is going on here, Lorenz? In one day, one man is shot to death and two others shot as well."

He picked up his medical bag. "I don't know, but it is bad." He hurried out the door as his wife was on the move preparing

160

the room for him.

Coming out of the house, Bren met him with the rig. He slid over as the doctor jumped into the seat and took the reins. Bren pointed. "Straight down the road."

The doctor broke the horse into a trot and moved out onto the road. When he reached the place where Miles knelt next to Caden, he pulled the rig to a stop, got out, and made a quick check of Caden. "Yes, he is alive. Get him on the back of the rig."

Rolling Caden carefully on his back, the three men lifted him and laid him on the bed of the rig. Bren jumped up on the back with his brother, while Miles led Caden's horse and followed as the doctor kept the buggy horse at a brisk walk back to his office.

Pulling around to the back door, they carried Caden in and laid him on the examination table. In the fully lit room they could see that Caden's shirt was a mass of dried and wet blood. His face was white and his body cold. The doctor turned to Bren and Miles and pointed. "In the waiting room, gentlemen."

"Will he be all right?" Bren shouted at him. "Will my brother be all right?"

"I will do what I can."

Miles put his arm across Bren's chest and

forced him out of the room. "Come on; let the doc work on him."

Bren sat down hard in a chair, his faced strained. He rubbed his hands hard across his face. He was close to tears. "I wish I hadn't said what I said before."

"It's okay, Bren, we were hoping for the best, knowing it could be worse."

"I know. I only said that because I was scared. Scared something like this had happened to him."

"He's a tough man, Bren, and the doc is a good one, let's keep our hopes up."

Bren leaned back in the chair pushing his legs out in front of him. He stared at the closed door behind which his brother lay between life and death. "I'm going to find the son of a bitch who did this and kill him."

Miles nodded. "I'll be right by your side."

"What do you think happened?"

Miles shook his head. "I don't know. Maybe it was a robbery."

"First we get cattle stolen, then Randy gets killed, now Cade. I think I've had about enough of this target on us. I'm going to find out where this gang is operating and wipe the lot of them out."

"Sounds like a good idea to me."

Dawn was breaking as sunlight streamed

through the windows of the doctor's waiting area. Bren was asleep in his chair and Miles was standing and staring out the window. It had been at least two hours since they brought Cade into the room. The length of time gave Miles hope that Cade was going to make it. If he was going to die, he would have by now; he had seen it before with wounded soldiers.

He spun around as the door opened and the doctor, looking worn and exhausted, came out. There was blood on his white apron as he walked toward them. Bren snapped awake and jumped to his feet.

The doctor sat down with a groan and removed his spectacles. "We now wait, gentlemen. The next forty-eight hours will tell. He has lost a lot of blood that his body must replenish and that can be a slow process. The bullet did not hit any major organs or his spine, which is a blessing in itself. A liver or kidney destroyed by a bullet does not regrow. He is strong, young, and in good physical condition, all points in his favor. It is the loss of blood I am most concerned with. If he had lain out there for another hour or two, he would have died."

Bren's expression was grim. "What happens now, doctor?"

"I will move him into a room here where

I can watch him for the next couple of days. If he makes it the forty-eight hours, he will be on his way to recovery. It will be slow after that, but if he lasts the forty-eight hours, he will live. It takes that much time to rebuild enough blood into his system to keep him alive."

"Then what?"

"At that time he can be moved home to recover. He will have more personal attention at home than I have time to give him here. Besides, patients heal quicker in a familiar environment."

Bren put out his hand. "Thank you, Doctor." Miles did the same. The doctor wearily shook their hands.

They turned at the sound of knocking on the front door. The doctor rose from his seat and answered it. It was Ita, followed by Rafe.

She walked in and looked at everyone. "We headed for town when no one came back this morning." The fear in her red eyes told of her long anguished night. "We saw everyone's horses outside. What happened?"

Miles took her hand. "Cade was shot. We found him in the road and moved him here in the doc's rig. The doctor just came out from working on him."

Ita turned her pain-wracked eyes to the

doctor. His face was a picture of kindness. "He is alive. He lost a lot of blood and that is the greatest danger right now. The wound was bad, but as I told the others, it missed all vital organs, that is very positive for his recovery. The next forty-eight hours will tell. His blood has to replenish and he has to build up enough strength to heal. If he makes it over that time, he will recover fully."

She looked into his eyes. "And if that doesn't happen?"

The doctor let out a pent-up breath. "He will die."

Ita swayed slightly and Miles helped her to sit down. She looked up at Miles. "Was it a robbery?"

The doctor answered, "His valuables and his money were still in his pockets. I will give them to you. It would be my guess that that rules out robbery."

"Then what was the reason?"

Miles shrugged. "We don't know, but Bren and me are going to find out what is going on around here."

Bren sat down next to her. "Miles and I are going to root these people out and put an end to this once and for all."

Rafe stepped forward. "I'd like to be in on that."

Ita looked up at him. "I know you would, Rafe, but with Bren and Miles gone and Cade . . ." She took in a shaking breath. "And Cade in this condition, I need you at the ranch."

"Sure, Ita, anything you want. You know I'll do whatever you need."

Ita smiled at Rafe and then looked at the doctor. "Can I see him?"

"Yes, for a bit. He's still unconscious, you understand."

Ita nodded and followed him into the room where Caden lay on his right side on the table. He was covered with several blankets to warm his body. She gasped at his white face and shallow breathing. She touched his face and felt coldness. She wiped a tear from her eye with a hand that trembled.

Leaning down by his ear she whispered, "I lost your pa and Aiden, I won't lose you too. You come back to your ma, you understand, Caden Patrick MacMahon. You come back to me."

CHAPTER NINE

Anna Stanford sat at the breakfast table across from her husband, who was ignoring her. She stared at him, wondering who this man was. She had never cared for his braggart ways and high opinion of himself. Those ill traits were still with him; however, there was now something else. There was now a meanness to him and a cockiness she had not seen before.

She had been attributing the changes to the influence of his older brother. She had not cared for Dillon the one time she had met him; however, she was beginning to understand, it may not be solely Dillon. This was possibly something that had lain under the surface of Arthur all along and was now emerging. Perhaps this was the real Arthur Stanford.

There were two distinct sides to his nature; one side was smiles and friendliness to someone's face, and then the hatred that spewed out when they were gone. Caden was a good example of that. To his face Arthur was pleasant, but behind his back Arthur was venomous against him. Last evening after Caden had left, Arthur had rampaged about the house raging over Caden's interference. It was frightening that he was more concerned about those two drunken men than about her and his daughter.

This morning he was particularly upset and on edge. He appeared very nervous and quick to snap harshly at her. Josephine avoided him altogether. Anna had made up her mind, at the first chance, she and Josephine would leave.

Last evening, he had ridden away just before dark and hadn't returned until late. He said not a word at his leaving or returning. She wanted some answers from him and was going to get them, though he would probably lie. There was a unending web of deceit and secretiveness to him of late.

"Arthur, where did you go last night?"

He glanced up at her. "I went out to check on the cattles. All this talk about outlaws and cattles stealing had me worried. I rode around the ranch. Everything was fine. I think this talk is a lot of old women afraid of the dark. There is no outlaw gang around here."

"Caden says there is."

He glared at her, but said nothing. She noticed that he flinched as if the name hurt. "Arthur, are you still angry with Caden?"

He had turned his face down toward the table and resumed eating. Now, his eyes snapped up to her with an angry expression. "He had no right interfering in my business."

"He was helping us."

"By running off the men my brother had sent to help with the ranch work?"

Anna's temper was rising. She was sick of hearing about his precious brother and how everything he did was wonderful. "They were not working on the ranch and you know it. They were often gone, and when they were here, they did nothing but drink and leer at Josephine. It scared me to death."

"I don't believe that for a second."

"So, *I* am the liar and *those* foul men and your *precious* brother are right? Your daughter's safety means nothing to you?" Her voice rose steadily in anger as she spoke.

"Of course it does."

"Well, obviously not that much. If not for Caden . . ."

Arthur jumped from the table, causing his

coffee to spill and his chair to tumble over backwards. He shouted at her, "Caden, Caden, I am tired of hearing about Caden. Those MacMahons think they are so big, so much, that they have the right to interfere in the lives of others. That Caden Mac-Mahon has no right to come onto my property and fire my men."

She was not afraid of him or his temper; she had never been afraid of him. "You dislike him because you embarrassed yourself with your bragging that night he was here."

For a moment she thought he would cross the table and strike her as his face turned red with rage. "I'm sick of people telling me how stupid I am." He turned and stormed for the door. "I have business with Dillon. I will be gone for a while." He slammed the door behind him.

Anna watched him through the window as he saddled his horse. Jo came into the kitchen and stood beside her mother. "I heard him shouting."

"Yes, it seems Caden is a very sore spot with him."

"I'm sure it is since Caden is a man and father is a coyote."

"What does that mean, a coyote?"

"It is an expression used out here for a man who is sneaky, underhanded, and cowardly. Like father is."

Anna realized that Josephine was right, Arthur was all of that. He and Dillon were up to something that was no good. She wondered about the outlaw activity, and it wasn't the first time she put Arthur and Dillon into those roles.

They continued to watch him as he finished saddling the horse and rode over the bridge and away. "Get your things packed, Josephine, we are leaving. I'm afraid he will come back with more of his brother's men and they may be worse than the first."

"What do you think is happening here, Mother?"

"I don't know, but I don't like what I'm seeing or what he has become. There are a lot of unanswered questions of late and I'm not sure I want to know the answers. I do fear that harm will come to us if we stay."

"Will we go to Ita's?"

Anna nodded. "Caden told us to, and we know we are welcome there, especially under the circumstances."

The two women hurriedly packed their bags and went out to the barn. Anna led one of the horses out of the corral and hitched it to the buggy. Jo shooed the second horse out of the corral and into the open pasture. They loaded into the buggy and left the yard. Driving over the bridge, Anna turned the horse to the left and up the road toward the main river road.

They drove for an hour, constantly looking back to make sure Arthur had not suddenly returned and was coming after them. Upon reaching the main road, Anna turned the horse to the right toward Niobrara.

"Where are you going, Mother? The Mac-Mahon home is the other direction."

"I want to pick up some things. I don't want to show up on Ita's doorstep empty-handed."

Ita left the doctor's office with Bren on one arm and Miles on the other supporting her. Rafe followed directly behind them. That the woman was badly shaken was evident. Bren sat down with her on a bench in the doctor's front yard. It was a pleasant spot with flowers growing around them.

"Ma, Miles and me are going to take a room at the hotel for the next two days to be close to Cade. We want to sit with him so when he comes around one of us will be there."

Ita nodded, her face pale and drawn. "That would be nice. I am staying, too."

"Are you sure you want to do that, Ma? You would be more comfortable at home."

"No. I would be worried sick at home. It takes too long to get from there to here. I would always be wondering if Caden made it through the night or if we'd lost him. I couldn't stand not knowing."

"Sure, Ma, we'll get you a room next to ours."

Miles and Rafe stood over them as they fell silent thinking back on the past several hours. As they lingered in the warm morning sun, the buggy with Anna and Jo rolled past. Jo pointed at them. "Mother, stop."

Anna pulled the buggy to a stop. Anna looked past her daughter to the four people in the garden. "Jo, that's the doctor's office. I wonder what happened." They got out of the buggy and walked toward them.

Anna looked down at her new friend. "Ita?"

Ita looked up at Anna. "Caden has been shot."

Jo put her hand over her mouth, stifling a scream. Tears instantly filled her eyes.

Anna gasped. "Oh, no, how is he?"

Bren answered, "Bad. The doctor says if he makes it through the next two days he'll pull through, but not unless."

Jo was crying. "What happened? When?"

Ita said, "He never came home from visiting you last evening. Bren and Miles went

173

out to look for him and found him in the road."

Bren broke in, "He had been shot in the back."

Between sobs Jo spoke in a shaky voice, "My father had brought two evil men to work on our place. He said they were ranch hands, but they weren't, they were drunken men and Mother and I were afraid of them. Cade gave them both a thrashing and ran them off the place. I wonder if they followed him and shot him."

Miles looked at her. "Can you tell me what these men looked like?"

Anna gave a brief description that could have fit half the men in the area.

"Why would your husband have men like that working on your ranch?"

Anna shook her head. "I don't know. I don't know about a lot of things that have been happening in our home lately. Ever since we came here and my husband re-joined his brother, there have been many unexplained matters."

Jo wiped her eyes. "Will I be able to see him?"

Miles held out his hand to her. "Come on, I'll take you in."

She put her hand in his. "Thank you."

Anna stayed with Ita. "Caden was doing

well when he left us last evening." Then, she shook her head. "Oh, Ita, something is very wrong. Caden wanted us to leave before we got hurt or one of my brother-in-law's *ranch hands* did something unspeakable to Josephine."

"Where are you headed, Anna?"

"Well, this is a bit embarrassing to say, but Caden had told us to go to your place where we would be safe."

Some of the fire that made Ita Mac-Mahon a strong, formidable woman returned. The initial shock of Caden's condition was wearing off and she was becoming angry. She lifted her chin and stiffened her back. "Don't be embarrassed, Caden was absolutely right. We have plenty of room and you must be safe. It sounds like your husband is playing some dangerous games with dangerous people."

"I don't know what he is playing, but if those two men are any indication, he is involved in something very bad."

Bren asked, "What do you know of his brother, Mrs. Stanford?"

"Very little, except I find the man altogether revolting. He runs or owns Stanfordville; I don't even know where it is except that Arthur always rides east when going there. His wife, Maude, is not what she appears to be. She puts on haughty airs; however, she doesn't fit into them. She is coarse and unrefined although she tries very hard to make herself appear to be socially elite. Whatever those two are doing, it must be criminal in nature and Arthur is with them in it."

"Are you sure your husband is involved with them?"

"I believe he is."

Miles reappeared with Jo. She was crying. "Mother, he looks so awful. He's so close to death."

Ita put her hand out to the girl who in turn took it in hers. "He's a tough one, honey. We are all hoping for the best. If he was a lesser man, he'd be dead already, but he's a MacMahon and that makes him tougher than any other man."

Jo smiled at her through the tears and leaned into her ear. "I hope to marry him."

Ita squeezed her hand and whispered back, "He wants to marry you too."

Ita turned her attention to Anna. "Go on out to the house and get settled in. I'm going to stay in town with Bren and Miles until we know Caden is out of the woods. We'll bring him home to mend. We'll be along in a couple of days.

"Rafe, will you please escort Anna and Jo home?"

"Of course. We'll be looking forward to you bringing Cade back home."

Ita smiled at him, her expression more confident. "And we will be too. If there's anything that needs my attention, you know where to find us."

Anna and Jo climbed back into the buggy and followed Rafe on his horse. Both sat in melancholy moods. Tears continued to trickle down Jo's cheeks. "Cade looked so close to death, Mother. Why would those men do such a thing?"

Anna was silent for a full minute. "It might not have been them."

Jo looked at her. "Who else then?"

"Your father left last night and was gone for several hours. He said he was checking the cattle, but now I wonder."

Chapter Ten

Henry had been assigned to the southeast line shack to work with George. At times they rode together making the rounds of their area; other times it was necessary to separate to cover more ground. Henry was determined to prevent any more events like the last rustling that resulted in Randy's death. The outlaws were not going to get one single OM beef, not on his watch.

George spoke little to Henry, keeping his thoughts to himself and not mentioning the incident in which Randy was killed. Henry had passed his fortieth birthday last year and wasn't much of a talker himself. The isolated life at the line shack suited him fine.

They made irregularly timed night checks of the cattle in addition to the day checks. The two men would take four-hour shifts in the night, waking the other to ride when the shift was over. They didn't want to set any kind of a pattern that could be used against them. Some nights they chose not to ride out at all. "Keep them confused" was Henry's statement to George.

Once a week, one of them would ride back to the main house and report to Rafe the conditions of that portion of range and the cattle. The ride in was considered the high point of the week. The man going got a chance to eat one of Sam's meals and not have to eat his own cooking.

The report was due this day and it was George's turn to ride in. He refused it, giving the opportunity to Henry. Henry took it without question. George had not awakened him for his night shift last night and had stayed out the whole night. Maybe he was tired now and wanted to be alone to grab some sleep. Sleeping during working hours was grounds for firing unless you had ridden nighthawk all night. Maybe George just preferred being alone. Whatever George's reason, Henry wasn't about to turn down a chance to ride in.

As he rode along the wagon rut road between the hills, he wondered why George had ridden guard all night. Why George hadn't awakened him for his shift. He didn't know George that well. Maybe it was his way of dealing with the loss of his partner. Henry shrugged and turned his thinking to his report for Rafe. Then he thought of Sam and a real meal. Maybe Sam had made pie. That alone was worth the ride.

Riding into the yard, he saw Rafe standing by a hitched buggy. He tied his horse to the corral rail and walked up to the foreman. Pointing at the rig, he grinned at Rafe. "Getting stylish in your old age. Too old to set a saddle, need a woman's rig?"

Rafe was not in a joking mood and gave Henry a hard glare. The two men had worked together on the ranch for years. Henry stopped grinning. "Either your milk was curdled this morning or something is wrong."

Rafe relaxed his glare. "Cade didn't come back last night. Miles and Bren went out looking for him around midnight and found him laying in the road up Niobrara way. He had been shot in the back."

"Oh, hell. How is he?"

"Bad. I didn't see him, but Miles said he looked like death. They got to him before he bled to death, but the doc says if he doesn't come around in the next two days, he won't make it."

Henry was at a loss for words. There wasn't a man on the place that didn't think the world of Caden. "Any idea who did it?"

Rafe shook his head. "No clue. Except,"

he pointed at the buggy, "Mrs. Stanford and her daughter happened by the doc's office. Cade had been up to see the girl and was apparently shot coming back from there. The girl said that Cade had run a couple of no-goods off their place that her fool of a father had hired and she thinks they did it. But, that's only a guess, we don't know for sure."

"We going to hunt 'em down?"

"Bren and Miles already have that covered. They're going to stay in town with Ita and wait to see if Cade pulls through. After that they're going to root this bunch out. I wanted to go along, but Ita needs me here."

Henry rubbed the whisker stubble on his jaw. "Two MacMahons are an army; I sure wouldn't want even one on my trail, let alone two."

Rafe looked at the buggy. "The Stanford women are going to stay here. Seems there's some bad business that her husband's wrapped up in and they're scared to be around him."

"Wonder if he's involved with the outlaws."

"I don't know, but there's been trouble aplenty the last couple of months and it's time to shut it down."

"Well, George and me have been keeping

181

an eye open round the clock. We've even took to riding nights to make sure no one slips in under cover of dark. Last night George was out all night."

"All night? What did he do that for?"

Henry shrugged. "I think he's still upset over Randy getting killed."

Rafe fell silent staring at the ground as if in deep thought. He looked back at Henry, "Something's not adding up over that business with Randy."

"Oh, yeah, how's that?"

"Carl bought Randy's Winchester. He said that when he checked it, there was an empty shell in the chamber."

"An empty shell? The only way you'd have an empty in the chamber is to have fired it."

"Exactly. Carl also said the magazine was down two cartridges. I've known Randy half my life; he would never let his gun down a single cartridge. He was no greenhorn, he'd fought Indians and he knew how dangerous a half-empty rifle could be. When he was done shooting he reloaded, it was a habit with him. He would never be down two cartridges and have an empty in the chamber unless he was in the middle of shooting."

"So, what are you saying, Rafe?"

"I'm saying Randy's the one who got the

shots off at the rustlers and was killed before he could jack the next shell in. I'm saying he's the one killed the rustler, not George. Randy hit what he shot at and he hit that rustler and killed him. I'd stake a month's wages on it."

"Okay, but George said *he* killed the rustler."

A voice came from behind them. "Henry, did you take a good look at Randy's body?"

They turned to see Sam walking up to them. "I heard what you were saying. I've been wracking my brain trying to remember what it was about Randy's body that wasn't right. Then, last night it hit me. Henry, how much blood was on Randy's shirt?"

Henry shrugged. "A ton."

"Yes, the front of his shirt was soaked in it, as was the front of his pants. I gave the wound a quick look; he had a big hole in the middle of him. There was hardly any blood on the back of him except where it seeped around."

Henry's eyes shifted around as he thought back to the moment when he and Sam found Randy on the bunk. They had bundled him up right away and he hadn't really looked, but he recalled that Sam had opened Randy's shirt and took a look. He had seen men shot before and got where

Sam was going with this. He steadied his gaze on Sam. "Randy was shot in the back?"

"I'd say so. Everything blew out the front of him. Randy was shot in the back at close range."

"That's crazy, Sam. Randy was facing the rustlers and shooting, he sure would never have turned his back on them."

Sam looked at Henry and then at Rafe. "There's only one way he could have been shot in the back. Only one person was behind him."

Henry suddenly turned angry. "You ain't accusing George, are you?"

"Just look at it, Henry. What else makes sense?"

Rafe held up his hand. "Let's go easy on this, boys. We can't accuse one of our men of a back-shooting murder on speculation. A lot of things could account for that."

"Maybe, but it doesn't hurt to keep it in mind. Henry, you be careful out there with him. Watch what you say and do, and don't trust him too far until we get some answers to this. He might be innocent, but if I'm right . . ." He left it at that.

Henry was thinking, his temper calming down. "Why would George say he killed the rustler then?"

"To cover his tracks?"

Rafe added, "There is one other thing that lends itself to that idea. Miles told me that when they confronted the rustlers in the saloon, George was quick to kill both of them. He said the man had a lightning draw and he shot them several times each. He wanted them dead." He looked at Henry. "Maybe you'd *better* be careful until we know for sure."

Henry rode back to the line shack, his mind a whirl of questions and doubts. He didn't want to believe that George was a murderer. Still, the questions about the empties in Randy's rifle and the bullet hole in Randy's body lent credence to the possibility of George's guilt. If it was true, they wouldn't wait for the law; they'd hang him themselves. He didn't want to rush to mistaken conclusions, though.

George had signed on for the spring gather. He wasn't the newest man, but hadn't been on long enough for anyone to really know him. He had pulled his weight, done his share, and never shirked a job. He was a good hand and all the men liked him. Still, what did they actually know about him?

Now, there was a cloud hanging over him.

If he had indeed killed Randy, then he had to be in league with the outlaw gang. If that was so, why would he turn around and kill the men he had killed Randy to protect? There was only one answer to that, to cover his own tracks, as Sam put it. That was a lot of killing just to keep his identity secret or, more likely, to avoid a MacMahon hanging. He knew some men were capable of cold-blooded actions, but George didn't seem the type.

New thoughts and ideas about George began to formulate in his mind. Maybe George was a spy. Could George be a spy for the outlaw gang? Was he here so he could direct the gang's rustling of Mac-Mahon cattle, of which there were thousands of head scattered over some fifty-thousand acres? Or was George a man in the wrong place at the wrong time and it just looked that way? He would play his cards close to the vest and watch.

George was in the line shack when Henry put his horse in the corral and stripped the tack off of him. He was feeling nervous not knowing what to expect. The questions caused him to look at George differently. He wasn't afraid of George. In a straight-on fight he gave as good as he got, but a man had no chance against a back shooter. If, in fact, George was a back shooter.

He pushed the shack door open and

stepped inside. "Hey, George, how's things going down here today."

"Same as always."

"No more rustlers?"

George shook his head. "Anything new from the house?"

"Yeah, Cade was shot last night."

George lurched forward in his chair. "What?"

"Yeah, Cade went out yesterday to visit his girl down on Verdigris Creek and on the way home he got bushwhacked. Shot in the back and left for dead."

George's face turned mean and red with anger. A deep rage was building under the surface. He glanced at Henry and saw him staring. "That really burns me up. Cade's a good man. How bad off is he?"

"They don't know. According to Rafe, the doctor said that if he makes it through the next couple of days, he'll pull through. He could die between now and then, though."

George settled back in his chair. He sat silent for several minutes before speaking again. "What are they going to do about it?"

"I don't know for sure, but Rafe said Miles and Bren are going hunting and put an end to this outlaw business once and for all." He studied George's face when he said it. His anger seemed to deepen.

Henry went on, "If I know the Mac-Mahons, they're about to turn this country upside down and shake it until all the rotten apples fall out of the tree. And if Cade dies, God help anyone who had a hand in it. There'll be blood on the ground."

The men sat in silence for several minutes. Henry watched George, wondering what was going on in his mind. That he was unhappy that Cade was shot was obvious, a reaction he would expect from anyone on the OM.

George looked at Henry. "Say, Henry, tomorrow is our day off. One of us has to stay here to keep an eye on the cattle, but I need to ride into town to buy a few things. Would you mind staying so I can go into town?"

"Not at all, especially since you let me take your turn to ride to the ranch today. I was thinking about doing some loafing and washing my clothes before they get up and walk away or skunks make a nest in them."

"Thanks, Henry. While I'm there I'll look in and see how Cade's doing."

CHAPTER ELEVEN

Thirty-six hours had gone by since Bren and Miles had brought Cade into the doctor's office. He had yet to regain consciousness, but the doctor was optimistic because Cade's color was returning to his skin and his breathing was deeper. He said those were good signs.

Not an hour passed when either Bren or Miles wasn't sitting by his side. Ita was in and out, constantly repeating her question, "has he come around yet," and having it consistently answered with a reluctant "no, not yet." She would sigh and sit down to watch his steady breathing, thankful that he still was breathing.

The doctor had been understanding of their need to be in the room with Caden and had kept them informed of Caden's changing condition. The family had known him in passing, but the last day and a half had bonded a friendship. His name was

189

Lorenz Keller, a German immigrant who still spoke with a strong German accent. He explained that he had been a surgeon for the Union during the war. He had operated on hundreds of wounds like Caden's and had saved many lives. That knowledge had helped to bolster their hope in Caden's recovery.

The clock in the front waiting area chimed one time. Bren and Miles were sitting in chairs dozing in and out of sleep. Caden opened his eyes and wondered at the strange surroundings. His mouth was bone dry and his throat hurt from lack of moisture. In fact he hurt all over. Slowly recollection came back to him. He had left Jo's and had just gotten onto the main river road. He had bent over to pull something out of his stirrup and then a sudden burst of pain and confusion. That was all he remembered. Now, he was here.

His eyes began to focus and he could see Miles and his brother sleeping in chairs across from him. Bren's head was leaning on the chair back and Miles had his arms folded across his chest with his chin down above them. A little bit of saliva was forming in Caden's mouth, enough to croak out, "Don't you two ever work?"

Miles' eyes snapped open and his head

jerked up. He looked around and then at Caden. Seeing his eyes open, he hit Bren with his elbow and jumped up. Bren's head came forward and he looked at his brother. A smile broke across his face as he leaped toward Caden.

Caden forced one side of his to mouth into a slight grin. "Just hanging around as usual."

Bren laughed. "Look who's talking Rip Van Winkle, you've been napping for two days."

Caden smacked his dry mouth. "I feel awful. Where am I?"

Miles squatted down so his face was level with Caden's. "You're at Doctor Keller's. We found you in the road, you had been shot. We weren't sure if you were going to pull through or not."

Bren ran out of the room and got Doctor Keller. Keller looked at his patient and smiled. "I see you have awoken, Caden. How do you feel?"

"Like dried bones in the desert that's been run over by a freight wagon."

"Good. Feeling pain is a good sign." He removed a short, slim glass tube from a cabinet and stuck it in Caden's mouth. "Do not move or speak for five minutes; I am taking the temperature of your body." He held his pocket watch in his hand and focused on it.

Bren stared at the thing in his brother's mouth. "Doctor Keller, what is that?"

"It is called a thermometer; it registers the body temperature. The body must be at a certain temperature to be healthy. It was invented by an English physician. Now hush, I am watching the time."

They watched in silence until the doctor closed his watch, removed the thermometer from Caden's mouth, and looked at it. "Ja, good. You are on your way to recovery, Caden."

Miles and Bren could not contain their joy and whooped and clapped their hands. They shook the doctor's hand and thanked him repeatedly.

"I am a very good surgeon, you know." Keller smiled with triumph.

"The best, Doctor Keller, the best." Bren shouted. "I'll go get Ma." He ran out of the office.

It was only a matter of minutes before Bren was back with his mother. She was breathing hard trying to keep up with him. She walked quickly into the room and beamed a smile as she looked at Caden's open eyes. He grinned through his cracked lips. "Hello, Ma."

Ita gently put her arms around him and hugged him. Tears were trickling from the corners of her eyes. "We were afraid we were going to lose you."

"How many times was I shot?"

"Just once," she answered.

"That's nothing; it would take at least twenty or thirty to kill a MacMahon."

Ita looked at the doctor. "When can we take him home?"

"A couple more days, I want to observe him to make sure there are no secondary infections or complications."

Caden turned his eyes up to the doctor. "I'm ready to ride."

"Nein! Nein!" Keller burst out. "No riding. No nothing for at least one month."

"Why so long?"

"You must understand, Caden, you have been shot. A large piece of lead has torn apart your insides. I had to suture several places in your intestines where the bullet tore holes in it. Holes in the intestine are very dangerous. If you tear open the sutures before the intestines heal, there will be seepages of partially digested food leaking into your body. This will poison you just as quickly as if you drank arsenic. You will die for certain. You will stay bedridden until I say otherwise. I will not allow you to undo my surgeries."

Ita looked at the doctor. "We will be sure to keep him down, Doctor." She turned her eyes to Caden. "You will do as the doctor says young man, do you understand?"

"Yes, ma'am. Is there any chance I can have a drink of water?"

Three days later Bren and Miles brought Caden home in a slowly driven wagon. Jo was at his side the second the wagon pulled in. He smiled at her and she gripped his hand and cried. Anna also shed a tear and welcomed him home. Most of the crew was on hand to greet him, and they all gave him a resounding cheer.

He was helped to his bed, much to his protests, which were ignored by the family. He complained of being treated like a baby and in turn was told to "stop acting like one then" by his mother. That cut his complaints short especially since it was said in front of Jo. Miles ordered him to stay put in bed, that they hadn't done all this work so he could run around and kill himself.

He admitted that he felt weak and didn't have the strength to get up anyway. He didn't like that he had to be waited on. He couldn't walk up to the cook shack so his meals would be brought to him. Ita did make one concession. She set up a lap table so he could sit up in bed for short periods and take care of the paperwork and accounts for the ranch. He could still take care of the payroll and meet all the operating needs of the ranch. That made him feel a bit more useful.

He had several long talks with Jo as she came often to sit by his bedside. He could see how worried she had been. They considered what her father was up to. He was hesitant to say that he suspected her father was linked to the outlaw gang through Dillon; however, she seemed to suspect it herself. He was glad she and Anna had come to the house.

She continued to fuss over him, which he took with patience and good humor. He felt unmanly not being able to manage things himself. He was wise enough to realize, though, that helping him was important to her, so he did not refuse her assistance.

Caden had been home for only two days and he was already getting restless with his confinement. Between his mother and Jo, he was kept from doing anything that would cause him more harm. He didn't like it, but he acquiesced. Most of the time he was too worn out and weak to resist, yet he would never admit it.

He was propped up in a half-sitting position working over some papers when Miles and Bren walked in. They stood over him grinning. Caden looked up at them and frowned. "What are you two grinning at? You look like foxes that just raided the chicken coup."

Bren's grin widened. "Just looking at a bedridden MacMahon. It's a rare sight, possibly never before seen. I was thinking of getting one of those photographers to come up and take a photograph of this and put it in a museum along with old bones and other rare sights."

"I won't be in this fix forever, little brother, and I do have a long memory. You might find your own self in a museum stuffed like a bear."

Miles chuckled. "Enjoy it, Cade. There ain't a man on this place wouldn't take a bullet if it meant having a pretty girl fussing over him. If I was twenty years younger, I'd shoot myself for it."

Caden could no longer hold down the grin. "Some men are just born lucky, I guess."

Miles' expression turned serious. "Bren and me are heading out now. We're going to try and get a lock on this outlaw gang."

"What are you going to do when you find them?"

"Considering the lost cattle, Randy's death, and your bushwhacking, I figure to kill the whole damn lot of them."

"I wish I was going with you."

"Well, get that notion right out of your thick skull. We need you up and healthy. You heed what that doc said about those leaking guts. I've seen soldiers get out of a hospital bed so they could go back and fight. I also seen them swell up and die a painful death that the surgeon couldn't undo. Just keep your tail in that bed."

"Yeah, I know." He thought for a second, then said, "Find that Stanfordville. Arthur Stanford is spending more time there than at home. His brother, Dillon, is there and after what I've seen and heard, I keep wondering if he isn't the same man you talked about before."

"The Dillon Stanford I knew was scum. I testified against him at the court martial. He hates my guts, but the feeling is mutual. Any idea where his town is?"

"Arthur told me it was a three-hour ride from his place and he indicated almost due east, maybe a little south."

"It shouldn't be too hard to locate once we get into that part of the country."

Bren and Miles shook hands with Caden and left the room. They discussed their intentions with Ita. She was concerned with their taking on a gang of murderers and thieves by themselves. She knew what kind of man Miles was and Bren was cut from the same cloth. If anything, it was the outlaws who should be afraid.

Loading their saddle bags with trail food and ammunition and tying bedrolls to the backs of their saddles, they mounted up and rode out of the ranch yard.

Mid-morning of the day after Miles and Bren left, Major O'Connor rode up to the house accompanied by two men. One man was dressed in a black suit that was now a light tan color from the layer of dust it had accumulated from the dry road. He was a bookish man whose strength appeared more academic than muscular, a man more at home with a ledger than a gun. He swatted at the dust clinging to his coat in a futile effort to clean it.

The second man wore the clothes of a range rider. He was a man of fifty, tall and straight. His eyes were brown and penetrating, peering at life over a gray-streaked, dark-brown mustache. He paid no attention to the trail dust that clung to him like a second skin. A Winchester was in the saddle scabbard and a Colt, snug in its holster, hung from the belt around his waist. His shirt was covered by a leather vest with a Bull Durham tag hanging from the side pocket.

Ita walked out of the house at the sound of the approaching horses. She waved at the Major. "Morning, Major, see you brought some guests."

The men dismounted. O'Connor gestured toward the man in the suit. "Mrs. Mac-Mahon, this is Harold Anderson, the new agent at the Agency. As you recall, I told you Smith and Adams have been arrested for thievery and a new agent would be appointed. This is the man."

Harold Anderson removed his hat and put his hand out to Ita. "A pleasure to meet you, Mrs. MacMahon. Major O'Connor has told me much about you."

Ita shook his hand. "Nice to meet you, Mr. Anderson. It will be good to have a decent man at the Agency for once."

"Well, thank you, Mrs. MacMahon. The Major has filled me in on the activities of my predecessors; I can assure you there will be no more of that while I am in charge."

"Glad to hear it."

"I would like to discuss the purchase of

some cattle while we are here, if that is all right with you."

Ita nodded. "You bet."

Ita's attention went to the tall man standing quietly beside the Major. O'Connor turned toward the man. "Mrs. MacMahon, this is U.S. Marshal Thomas Prideux, from Yankton. He's here to investigate the recent outlaw activity."

Marshal Prideux swept his hat off his head and extended his hand. "Mrs. MacMahon."

Ita shook his hand. "Nice to see you, Marshal. We've had a lot of it in the last couple of months."

"Yes, ma'am. I was talking to Jason Young and a couple of the other ranchers a while back. They have been having a hard time with the outlaws. Unfortunately, I don't have a lot of time to pursue them."

"It's a big country all right. Cattle rustlers made off with some of our cattle a couple of weeks back and killed one of our men in the process. Then, last Saturday night my son was bushwhacked, shot in the back and left for dead."

O'Connor's expression fell in shock. "Which son was shot?"

"Caden."

"How is he?"

"He pulled through, but he's laid up in

bed, doctor's orders. He doesn't like it none, but we're making him behave himself."

"That's certainly a relief to hear."

Prideux agreed. "That is good to hear. Was it the outlaws, do you think?"

Ita shrugged. "Could be, but we're not certain. Seems Caden had a run in with a couple of no-goods earlier that day. It could have been them as well."

"I would like to talk to your son, if I might."

"Certainly. Come on in, got coffee on the stove." She led them into the house.

She put cups on the table for each of them and filled them from the blue pot. She poured a cup for Caden and led the marshal to his room. Caden was concentrating on his paperwork when she walked in with the marshal.

She handed Caden the cup. "This is Marshal Prideux out of Yankton; he'd like to talk to you about this outlaw business."

Caden took the cup in his left hand and extended his right. "Pleasure to meet you, Marshal." The men shook hands.

Ita turned to go out. "I'll let you two discuss your business while I talk cattle with the Major and the new agent." She left them alone in the room.

Caden gestured to a chair. "Pull up a seat, Marshal. I feel kind of foolish laying around like this, but when you have two women hovering over you, you don't have much choice."

Prideux grinned. "Bullet wounds shouldn't be taken lightly and never dispute a woman intent on protecting you. It can get you killed. Do you mind if I call you Caden?"

"Not at all. What can I help you with?"

"I'm looking into the rash of outlawry down this way. I'm closer than the marshal in Omaha so it fell to me, but if it gets bad enough, I'll bring him in. I've gotten bits and pieces of information, but nothing I can use for a lead. Tell me what you know about it." He drank from his cup as he waited for Caden to answer.

"Jason said he had talked with you earlier. There's not much to tell. Jason told me that the rustling was most active south and east of the reservation. Then, last week a stage was held up between Niobrara and St. Helena, which means they're moving to the north now. Stages have been held up all along the Missouri River road; my guess is, it's based somewhere around Logan Valley."

"That's the information I'm getting as well. It was the robbery of that stage by St.

Helena, and the death of the shotgun guard, that brought me down here. I heard you folks had some trouble too, so that's why I thought to come and see what you could tell me."

"There's a man name of Dillon Stanford that seems to be someone prominent in a town called Stanfordville. I understand it's named after him. There are two ladies staying with us, a mother and daughter; the husband and father is Arthur Stanford and he spends a great deal of time in Stanfordville. His brother is this Dillon. I'm thinking Arthur has something to do with the outlaws."

"Really, what leads you to that?"

"The ladies came here because they no longer feel safe around him and the caliber of men he has been bringing to work on his ranch. Personally, I think his ranch is only a front for some other business. He knows nothing of cattle and never works the place."

Prideux pulled at his mustache. "Interesting. So, you think he's not a cattleman at all?"

Caden shook his head. "The family came from Minnesota a few months back where he ran a store. Dillon set him up with the ranch."

"So, you think Dillon has a reason for setting Arthur up with a false front?"

"That's my suspicion. The other day I was talking to him and he used the word 'brigands' to describe outlaws."

Prideux's eyebrows lifted. "Brigands? I haven't heard that word since I left Tennessee."

"It's not a common term out here. I once met a couple of Kentuckians who used the word 'brigands.' They said it was a word used to describe robbers and murderers on the Natchez Trace. That's what struck me when Arthur used the word."

"Yes, Natchez Under the Hill, it's called. It's the road through the thick woods that's crawling with highwaymen, bandits, killers, and robbers. There were some mean men and meaner gangs that prowled that road like a herd of panthers. They were called brigands. The law finally started closing the noose on them and a lot of them left for other parts of the country. I haven't heard that word used in a long time; it's not a term a western man would use or even a man from Minnesota."

The marshal fell into deep thought. Caden watched, expecting him to say something. After a minute he looked at Caden. "I'm wondering if this Arthur and Dillon might not have been a couple of those brigands that scattered. This outlaw business started what, a couple months ago? About the same time you say Arthur Stanford arrived here."

"Yes, about that time. That's when the worst of it started with the robberies to the east of here. Do you think there might be a connection with the Stanfords and the Natchez gangs?"

"I'm sure thinking it. I've got a good friend who still lives in Tennessee. He's on in years now, but he was a hell-on-wheels lawman in his day. He would know every outlaw or brigand who ever worked the Trace. I'm going to wire him and see if he ever heard of Dillon and Arthur Stanford."

"I'd like to know about that myself. My brother and uncle are heading out that way right now looking for their base of operation."

Prideux leaned forward in his chair and gave Caden a hard look. "That's pretty dangerous business, looking for outlaws. That's best left to the law."

"Meaning no disrespect, Marshal, but the law is spread pretty thin out here and if we waited for a lawman every time we had trouble, we'd have been wiped out a long time ago. We take care of own affairs."

Prideux relaxed and resigned himself to the statement. "You're right. That's how it's been out here for a long time. Law is thin or nonexistent, still, if you don't understand outlaws . . ."

"Miles rode scout in the Sioux wars. He rode scout against the Comanche at Red River and Palo Duro Canyon. He was marshal in Wichita and North Platte. He can take care of himself."

Prideux nodded his understanding. "A former lawman. Well, that does paint the horse a different color."

"Miles also knew a Dillon Stanford in the Army. He said Stanford was arrested for robbing the bodies of dead soldiers. He was court martialed and sent to prison for five years. When he got out, he hung around Yankton for a while and then disappeared around '70 or '71. He said Dillon Stanford was scum."

"Well, that *is* interesting, sounds like something a Natchez brigand would do. I wasn't here until '73 so I wouldn't have known him. I'll see what I can find out and get back to you. If it proves out that these Stanfords are Natchez escapees, I'll be riding down Logan Valley way myself."

"Miles is anxious to find out if this Dillon Stanford is the same one he knew."

Prideux stood up and shook Caden's hand. "I'll let you know what I find out."

The marshal walked out the door. As soon as he was out Anna stepped quickly into the room. Her face was drawn and her eyes reflected fear. Caden looked at her. "What's wrong, Mrs. Stanford, you look troubled."

"I heard what the marshal was saying. I had not thought about it before, but what the two of you were saying made me think. Arthur told me he was born and raised in Missouri; his parents had died when he was young. One day, years ago, I found in his papers an old ticket from a Mississippi River steamboat out of Natchez, Mississippi, and a yellowed newspaper clipping about a criminal gang called the Bruells. At the time I saw no connection with it to him and paid it no further mind. Now, I have to wonder if he really did come from Missouri. Maybe he is from Mississippi or Tennessee and had been associated with criminals before he moved north, that he has lied to me all these years."

"The ticket might have been a remembrance of a trip he took in his youth."

"And the newspaper clipping? Why save a newspaper article about a criminal gang?"

Caden shrugged. "I don't know."

"He has changed so since we came here and he has reunited with his brother. I don't even know him anymore. Those men he had

207

at the ranch. The way he now talks and the things he says make me think he had a very different life from a shopkeeper at one time."

She hesitated for a second, absently wringing her hands together. "He does not like you, Caden. He rode away that night after you left. He said he was checking cattle, but I don't believe him. I do not believe anything he says anymore. Caden, I believe he is the one who shot you."

CHAPTER TWELVE

Miles and Bren rode from west to east asking along the way for the location of Stanfordville. No one seemed to know of it or was unwilling to say if they did. They thought it unusual that a town would be unknown to everyone. Someone should have at least heard of it if not actually having been there. Bren figured it was a matter like a town bully; most people pretended he wasn't there in hopes he wouldn't pick on them. Stanfordville was the bully people were afraid of.

An old buffalo hunter in a saloon in the Plainview settlement knew of its location. He said it wasn't a friendly town, that the folks who ran the stores and shops were too scared to talk to anyone and a bunch of rough characters hung around doing nothing but scaring folks. He had been there twice and thought it a good place to avoid.

He said that Stanfordville was owned lock,

stock, and barrel by some oiled-down slick named Stanford who reminded him of a Mississippi riverboat gambler. The town was between the Logan and Plum valleys on the Elkhorn River. He went on to explain that most folks living around there by-passed it in favor of Logan Valley or Curlew to get supplies. No one in their right mind went to Stanfordville.

The old man said there was no town there at all up until about eight years ago. His understanding was that Stanford talked people into relocating there and building a town. He owned the land and made a lot of great promises of prosperity to all who joined him. He built the town by selling buildings or lots to businessmen. Then, a couple of years back Stanford showed his true colors and claimed ownership of the town. He used his hired thugs to enforce his rule and those that had built the town were his prisoners. Now, there was a batch of outlaws hanging around. He didn't know much more other than that.

Miles told him that everyone they asked claimed not to know about the place. The hunter said the settlers in the area were afraid of being raided and killed so they probably wouldn't want to say anything in case it came back on them. It was a bad place, but if they insisted on going up there, they needed to ride northeast, and then follow the Elkhorn River north and they'd find it. *"Don't say I didn't warn you,"* was his parting comment.

They rode on following the old hunter's directions, which brought them to the Elkhorn River. They followed the river north and found Stanfordville spread out on a level stretch of land along the river. A huge sign mounted on two posts set in the ground had the single word "Stanfordville" written boldly across its face.

The buildings were fairly new. Some still had the orange sheen of mill-dried lumber; others were painted. They were quick to note that there were no children or women visible. No farm wagons were parked in front of the stores. There were only saddled horses at the rails and men loafing about.

Miles sized the town up right away. This was an outlaw town. It had the kind of shops and stores that most towns had, indicating that at one time it had been a family town. That was no longer the case; this was not a town he would want his family in. The businesses had to be suffering from lack of buyers. Outlaws didn't buy, they took.

They rode slowly down the main street

taking in the layout. They were quickly becoming the focus of attention by the loafers on the boardwalk. There were dry goods stores, a gun shop, tobacco and liquor, and a cluster of others that appeared empty. The saloons were the only places that seemed to be busy.

Two additional streets ran parallel to the main street, one on the west side and one on the east. These streets were connected to the main street by short alleys that separated the main street businesses in groups of six or eight buildings. The secondary streets held the livery barn, stables, storage buildings, and a large building that had probably once been intended for a town meeting hall, but was now vacant.

Bren let his eyes rove over the scene without appearing to be seriously studying the town. "What do you make of it, Miles?"

"It's an outlaw town just like the old man said."

Bren nodded. "You can feel it in the air. This isn't a town people make a trip to for supplies, like we do in Niobrara."

Miles returned an icy look from a man who was glaring hard at him. "Not if they value their lives."

"If Jo's pa spends his time here, then I

guess that pretty much sums up what he is."

"Yeah, an outlaw. Him and his brother both, they run the town. I want to get a look at this Dillon. I'm betting the oiled-down slick the old man was talking about and the Dillon Stanford I knew are one in the same."

Bren turned his head and looked through the window of a food store with no customers in it. "What I don't understand is how this was once a family town, and then all of a sudden it's an outlaw town. How does that happen?"

"It happened in Texas with Lampasas and the Horrell family, and again in Eagle Pass with King Fisher, to name only two. A gang of outlaws moves in and takes over. Here it's the Stanfords, but this is different because it was intended to be an outlaw town. The fact was hidden from the men who were encouraged to move in and build stores and businesses. The hidden plan was to profit off them. Dillon probably owns or holds the notes on all of these businesses. Then, when the time was right, he brought in the outlaws and set up his criminal headquarters here. Those with their money locked up in their stores and homes were trapped."

"Like a long-range plan?"

"You got it."

"That's slimy."

"Just like Dillon Stanford. Now, you see why I hate this man. Robbing dead soldiers or robbing merchants, it's all the same to him."

"Okay, we found them, now what?"

"I want to know more about the operation. How many outlaws we are up against and where Dillon holds court. It's like a big rattler; it's deadly, but it's only as strong as its head. You cut the head off and the rest of it dies even if it's six feet long. We get rid of Dillon and his brother and the rest of them will clear out. Hired outlaws don't stick around or put up a fight when there's no one to pay them for it."

They continued on. Miles pointed at another store with no customers in it. "Let's see how some of the locals feel about this place." They dismounted, tied their horses to an empty hitch rail, and went in the store.

A middle-aged man with a weary face looked at them in surprise from behind his counter. Miles greeted him in a friendly manner. The man was clearly nervous and returned the greeting hesitantly.

"Miles MacMahon. We've come to take Dillon Stanford apart. Where can we find him?"

The store man was unable to speak at first, surprised by the stranger's abrupt announcement. He finally found his voice. "That's dangerous talk around here, Mr. MacMahon. You could get killed for saying that."

"We're dangerous men, sir, and we've had enough of Dillon Stanford stealing our cattle and shooting our people. We've come to put a stop to it."

Bren looked around the store. "Looks like he's got this town sewn up."

The man flicked his eyes fearfully from side-to-side as if afraid someone was listening. He leaned toward them and whispered, "He does, and he enforces it with his hired killers. Everyone here is terrified to cross them. This was once a decent town, but . . ." He stopped mid-sentence, straightened, and spoke in a loud voice, "Sorry, gentlemen, we've run out of smoking tobacco, try the tobacco store down the row."

Miles and Bren turned to see two of Stanford's outlaws standing inside the store glaring at them in an attempt to intimidate. Miles smiled at the store man. "Thanks, we'll try that store."

As they walked toward the door the men blocked their exit. "New in town?" asked one.

Miles and Bren squared up in front of the two. Miles gave a cold smile. "You seem to be blocking our way."

"You didn't answer my question."

"That's because it's none of your business what we're doing. Now, get out of our way or they can scoop you up with a manure shovel." Miles flipped the loop off his Colt's hammer as did Bren.

The outlaws hesitated. They were used to successfully bullying the townspeople and had never been challenged. They each sidestepped, opening a gap between them. "Tell your boss that Miles MacMahon's looking for him." He and Bren shoved them out of the way as they passed between them and out to their horses.

Bren grinned. "I guess they don't like strangers in their town."

"It does appear that way. Let's talk to the hostler at the livery. They always know everything that's going on." They rode toward the livery at the end of the west side back street as the two outlaws stepped outside the store and watched them. The outlaws then turned and hurried down the boardwalk to a saloon and disappeared into it.

The store man cautiously left his store and went into the shop next to him. He began there to spread the word that two tough men were in town hunting for Dillon Stanford. He hoped they succeeded in their quest.

Riding into the livery barn they were met by the hostler. He smiled at them. "Plan on staying? Gotta warn you, it's a dangerous town."

They remained mounted. Miles smiled back. "I understand Dillon Stanford runs this town."

The man's smile faded. "He does that. Backs it with that scum of the earth too. It's a shame, it started out a nice town, but I reckon that was Stanford's plan all along. Get us in and then rob us blind."

"How do folks around here feel about him?"

"Well, let's put it this way, if he was on fire we'd all throw coal oil on him. Everyone hates his guts and that lousy brother of his too. He's probably worse; he's a weak sister, but because of his big brother, he thinks he can throw his weight around. Everyone's too scared of the thugs to challenge him so he pushes it. He only showed up a couple months back."

"Must make it kind of hard on business."

"It does that. No one comes to buy anymore, but Stanford keeps collecting his money from us. We're all broke paying out with nothing coming in, but he doesn't care."

"How would you all feel if he was gone?"

The hostler's face broke into a wide smile. "Why, we'd throw the biggest shee-bang this country ever saw."

Miles grinned. "Where can we find him?"

"Stanford's Crystal Queen. Can't miss it, it's the biggest, fanciest place on the main street."

"Guess we'll wander up that way and pay him a visit. Tell the fiddler to get tuned up." They rode out of the barn while the hostler watched them leave.

In the middle of the row was a saloon that was twice the size of the others. It had two stories with windows lining the upper floor. The outside had ornate woodwork, glass windows, and glass in the double doors. A sign painted in scripted green letters read *Stanford's Crystal Queen.* Miles pulled to a stop in front of it. "Here's where we find the rattler's head."

They reined their horses to an opening at the hitch rail and dismounted. Miles looked the place over. "You know what this reminds me of, Bren? It reminds me of New Orleans or a Mississippi riverboat with a name like that."

"Have you been there?"

"A time or two. I rode a riverboat from Arkansas to New Orleans once and this is the kind of sign and building you see down in that country. I don't know where Dillon came from, but he wasn't born in the west, and if I recall right he did have a bit of the south to his speech."

Opening the left side of the twin doors, Miles kept his right hand close to the butt of his Colt. He entered the room with Bren behind him. The walls of the saloon were decorated in scrolled woodwork and paintings. A hardwood bar, polished to a high shine, reflected the men lined up at it. A shiny brass rail ran just above the floor in front of the bar.

The room was busy with men drinking and playing games of chance. The ball on a roulette wheel rattled while the man behind it called out the results. A faro table was against the far wall with the dealer snapping out cards to two players. Poker cards rustled as they were shuffled and dealt, and a low din of mixed voices floated through the room. Cigar and cigarette smoke wafted on the air, while girls in bright dresses made their way among the men, touching them and making brief comments as they passed. In turn the men looked back at them and smiled or leered.

Miles noted that most of the men in the room were not working men. There were no farmers or stockmen. A few of the men looked like those that could be found in any saloon; they weren't outlaws, maybe locals. The majority were an unkempt lot that were out of place in a saloon that had the appearance of a big city establishment catering to a wealthy clientele. Dillon might wish it was New Orleans, but it was a little town in Nebraska that he had built and populated with outlaws. The décor of the place could not change that.

They moved up to the bar under the watchful eyes of the men in the room. The barkeep stood in front of them. Miles held up two fingers. The barman set down two glasses and filled them from a whiskey bottle. Miles dropped a pair of coins on the bar that the man scooped up. They both turned to watch the room.

A girl came up to Bren and smiled. "Hello."

Miles looked at her. "Not now, honey, he's busy."

"How about you, are you busy?"

"Yeah, I'm busy looking for Dillon."

The girl's smile disappeared as she quickly moved away. The barkeep came up behind them. "Stanford doesn't just see anyone."

Miles turned back toward him. "Why is that?"

"Because he's a busy man."

"Runs this town, does he?"

"It's his town, yes. He owns everything in it."

Miles tossed his drink down and pointed at the glass. The man refilled it. "And everyone in it?"

The barkeep's expression turned sour. He spoke under his breath, "Something like that." He leaned in closer. "A word to the wise, get out while you can." He turned away and walked down the bar to another customer.

Miles spoke to Bren without looking at him. "Everyone's scared, like the old man said."

"They are scared all right and I can see why."

Miles gestured toward a closed door in the back of the room. "That's his office there." As he said it a woman of forty-some years walked out of the room. She was wearing an expensive dress and her red hair was pinned high on her head. She walked like she considered herself an aristocrat. Back straight, nose slightly lifted, she presented an air of arrogance.

221

The girl Miles had sent away hurried up to the woman and whispered something to her and glanced in the direction of Miles and Bren. The woman squinted her eyes to see through the smoke as she looked across the room. She nodded and walked toward them.

She stopped in front of Miles. "I understand you are looking for Mr. Stanford. Why?"

Miles grinned at her. She was putting on airs and doing it badly. Ten-plus years had etched their way across her face since the last time he had seen her, but her blue eyes remained as hard as ever. "Hello, Kelly, still giving the Irish a bad name I see."

The woman's face fell in shock. Her eyes opened wide in horror at being recognized by someone who could reveal the truth about her past. She fought to regain her composure. "You have me confused with someone else, sir. My name is Maude Stanford; I have no idea who this Kelly is."

"Sure, keep telling everyone that. Where's Dillon?"

"Why?"

"Just wanted to say hello, it's been a long time since Yankton. I was hoping prison had done him some good, but it doesn't look like it."

He had the attention of the men in the room as they watched and listened. Those that looked like locals were particularly paying attention.

The woman glared at him trying to remember his face, and then her eyes filled with recognition. "Miles *MacMahon*. You have your nerve showing up here."

"No, actually, you people have your nerve stealing MacMahon cattle."

"I have no idea what you are talking about."

"Sure you do. I'm here to put a stop to it."

Bren added, "And I want the one who put a bullet in my brother's back."

The woman looked at Bren and was about to speak when she heard the office door open in the quiet room. The roulette wheel was silent and the cards were on the tables. She closed her mouth and looked back.

A man dressed in a suit walked out of the office toward them. It was apparent he had been in a fight as he had a black eye and scabbed-over lips. He stopped beside them and looked at the woman. "Is there a problem here, Maude?"

Snapping her chin toward Miles, she sneered, "Yes, Art, there is a problem. This man is trying to see Dillon and attempting to make a scene."

Miles gave the man a thin smile. "Looks like you got the short end of a fight, *Art*? Is that short for Arthur? I'm Miles Mac-Mahon; I think you know my nephew."

Art's eyes narrowed. "I think you need to leave."

"After I see Dillon. I have a message for him, but the yellowbelly is probably hiding."

"You can give it to me."

"No, I don't think so. I don't go through underlings or prostitutes."

The woman's face became an ugly sneer. Art turned toward four men at a table and jerked his head at them. "These men will escort you both out."

Art and Maude walked back across the room, leaving the four men to face Miles and Bren. "Let's go," the foremost man sneered. "Mr. Stanford wants you out."

Without a warning Miles snapped a hard right fist into the man's solar plexus, dropping him to the floor. Bren threw a punch in the face of the next man, breaking his nose. He clasped his hands over his face and staggered backwards.

The two outlaws behind the fallen men went for their guns. Miles and Bren both drew at the same time. There was less than six feet between them and the outlaws when they fired. Miles and Bren each fired two shots. The men fell to the floor.

With guns raised, Miles and Bren backed their way to the door. Men had risen to their feet like they wanted to attack, but none wanted to rush the guns of two men who had already proved they would shoot. Easing out of the door, they made it to their horses. Men began to run out of the various saloons and alleys toward them. Firing shots at the oncoming outlaws caused them to duck back into the buildings and alleys for cover. One at a time Miles, and then Bren, mounted while the other held cover. They kicked their horses into a gallop as they raced of out of town, throwing shots at the outlaws on the sides of the street as they flew past them.

A mile out of town they stopped in a grove of trees and watched their back-trail as they reloaded their pistols. Seeing no pursuit after fifteen minutes, they dismounted. Bren grinned at Miles. "That was fun."

"I thought so. We did find out a few important things. The *Dillon* running this town and the outlaw gang is the same one I knew, Kelly being here proves that. Jo's father is part of it. We reduced their ranks by two, maybe three, that one with the broken nose won't be much good for a while. All in all, I think it went well."

"They at least know now that pushing MacMahons is bad for your health."

Miles grinned. "That's a polite way of putting it."

"That Art looked like he took a beating from someone."

"Hard to imagine anyone beating him up, what with that pleasant personality he has."

"Okay, Miles, now what?"

"I still want to take this gang apart and put an end to Dillon Stanford's control. We've learned that the townspeople are not backing him, just the opposite; they'd like to see him dead. I want to do some riding around and see if anyone will talk about the gang. We need to find out how they are operating and maybe, if we're lucky, nail a few more of them."

"So, we're going to stick around and make trouble for them?"

"As much as we can."

"Good. I'm sure one of them is responsible for shooting Cade and I want the chance to put a bullet in whoever did it."

Miles thought silently for a few seconds before speaking. "Do you recall Cade saying Dillon had a ranch with cattle and horses?"

Bren nodded. "Yeah, he said something like that."

"Let's find it. I'd like to see what his brand is and if there are other brands mixed in with them."

"Like an O-M?"

"Yeah, like an O-M."

CHAPTER THIRTEEN

Marshal Prideux rode back to the Mac-Mahon house three days after he left. He had stayed in Niobrara until receiving answers to his telegrams. He rode in with the telegrams in his pocket. Tying his horse to the corral, he walked to the house, climbed the steps, and knocked on the door.

Ita opened the door. "Marshal Prideux, please come in. Caden said you might be coming back."

The marshal pulled off his hat. "Good day, Mrs. MacMahon. Yes, I have information from my friend in Tennessee. I also have an interesting telegram from a former marshal of Judge Parker's in the Indian Territory. I told Caden I would let him know what I learned."

"We would all like to hear that, Marshal. Let's go to Caden's room and we can all listen."

"How is Caden's recovery?"

"Like trying to keep a greased piggie in a metal bucket. He's going a little crazy with cabin fever."

Caden was talking with Jo when Ita walked in with the marshal. Caden looked at him and smiled. "Marshal Prideux, good to see you again. Did you learn anything?"

Prideux looked at Jo and hesitated. Anna then walked into the room and he looked nervously at her. He understood why the two women were at the house and he was reluctant to say what he had learned in front of them.

Anna sensed his hesitation. "Please, Marshal, go ahead with what you have to say. I need to know if Arthur has a criminal past and if he has returned to that past. I thoroughly distrust him and would like to know the truth."

Prideux nodded. "Yes, ma'am, I understand."

He pulled the first telegram out of his pocket. "This is one from my friend in Tennessee. He says that there was a Natchez Under the Hill gang, a vicious lot of murderers, led by two brothers and two cousins, all named Bruell. They operated along the Mississippi stretch of the Trace. He said that the law was closing in on them. They had ambushed the gang and killed several, but the Bruells escaped and disappeared from that part of the country. The brothers were Dillon and Art. The cousins were Ed and George."

The room was silent as they listened. Anna appeared to be in a daze as her husband's past was revealed. The name of Bruell in the yellowed newspaper article took on a new and frightening significance. She suddenly felt ill. Ita glanced at her and noticed her loss of color.

Prideux looked at Anna. "I'm sorry, Mrs. Stanford, but it appears your husband's real name is Bruell, as is his brother's. Both were leaders of that Mississippi gang."

Anna nodded. "I suspected something was wrong when Arthur rejoined his brother and changed so much. Years ago I found an old newspaper clipping in his papers about an outlaw gang by the name of Bruell. I did not know what it meant then, but now it makes sense. It was about him."

"Yes, it appears so, Mrs. Stanford. I am sorry."

Caden looked at Anna and then to the marshal. "So, Art and Dillon are Bruells. Miles had said that Dillon had taken up with a woman named Kelly, she was a prost—" He caught himself and glanced at the women. "A woman of ill repute. They left Yankton together in '70 or '71; he had word that Dillon had won land in a poker game. I wonder if that's when Stanfordville began."

Anna was still looking ill when she added, "That would make sense about Dillon. I did not like him the one time I met him and his wife . . . I guessed there was something unclean about her. She would fit the Kelly woman, even though she calls herself Maude now."

"Yes, ma'am." Prideux gave her a sad look. "Putting this all together, I believe the Bruells left Mississippi and split up. Dillon went to Dakota and joined the Army, which would be a good place to hide. That is until he couldn't control his thieving ways. Art obviously went to Minnesota. They both changed their names to Stanford."

"What about Ed and George?" Caden asked.

"My friend gave me the name of a marshal who used to ride for Judge Parker, but now he's an old man living in Dodge City. From him I learned that he captured Ed and George Bruell in the Indian Territory, where they had murdered a freighter and stolen the goods in his wagon. They were suspected of other murders as well. They escaped custody, killing a guard in the process. They were not heard from again in the Territory.

"The conclusion I am drawing from all this is that the Bruells have reunited to rebuild their outlaw gang here in Nebraska. I believe it is operated out of Stanfordville. We know where Dillon and Art now are, but have you heard of George or Ed?"

Caden exchanged a concerned look with his mother. Rafe had talked to them both about Sam's suspicions regarding George Carson. He told them what Carl had said concerning Randy's rifle and what Henry had said about George's all-night ride. He and Ita had thought that it sounded and looked suspicious, but agreed with Rafe that they should not jump to conclusions. With this new information, it was all adding up to an uncomfortable conclusion. If George Carson was George Bruell, and he had murdered Randy, it was a MacMahon affair and they would deal with George in their own way.

Caden shook his head. "No. We just know about Arthur and Dillon. I agree with you, though, that they seem to have rebanded. There have been too many crimes lately in one area to be anything else."

"Well, then, I believe I will take a ride to Stanfordville. I have learned where it's located." He said good-bye to the ladies and once again told Anna he was sorry for the bad news he had brought her. Ita walked him out.

Anna went to her room and sat on the edge of the bed looking stunned. Jo sat down next to her and they held hands. Ita walked back to Caden's room and looked in at the women as she passed. "I'm sorry, Anna."

Anna shook her head. "Twenty years I have been married to him. Twenty years of a lie, even our name is a lie. There was much about him I didn't like, but at one time I did fall in love with him. It was all a lie."

Jo squeezed her mother's hand. "We will get through this together, Mother."

Anna smiled at her daughter with tears glistening in her eyes. "Yes, we will, my dear one."

Ita moved away from the women and went into Caden's room. "Well?"

Caden scowled. "I think we have a traitor in our midst. A murderer and a spy, whose purpose for being here was to help his cousins steal our cattle. Randy got in the way."

Ita was angry. "I want him strung up."

"I do too, but we have nothing to prove it. Hanging a guilty man caught in the act is one thing, but I won't hang a man on

233

suspicion. Ma, send Rafe and Sam in here, please."

Ita left the room while Caden contemplated how to handle the situation with George. They had to know for sure. He was hoping Rafe or Sam might have an idea.

Half an hour passed before Caden heard footsteps coming toward his room. Ita entered followed by Rafe and Sam. Rafe asked, "Ita told us what the marshal said. What do you want to do?"

"We need proof. We have a lot of suspicion, but no proof. Sam, tell me about Randy's body."

"I gave the wound a quick look, but Henry and I didn't spend a lot of time looking at Randy since he was already gone. We rolled him up and brought him back. It was the blood and the big hole in the front of him that kept nagging at me. Then, I figured it out. All of it was in the front, like when a bullet makes a small entry hole and then blows everything out when it exits the other side. Randy was shot in the back, not in the front. Then, there was the business about the empty shell in Randy's rifle chamber. It adds up."

Caden considered the information. "I was thinking about something while waiting for you. Remember Miles thought George had

234

been too quick to kill those rustlers?"

Rafe shrugged. "Sure, but I wasn't there."

"Maybe he wanted to shut them up before they could say anything."

"We had thought about that too."

"Adding to that, we caught the last one as he tried to make a run for it. Miles was going to hang him, but George wasn't sure if the man we had was actually one of the rustlers. The man we had kept denying any knowledge of the rustling, said he was just in town and got scared and ran. But he kept looking at George and even pleading with him. I wonder if that wasn't Ed we had."

"It sounds like George was covering for himself by killing the first ones, but then he protected his brother."

"That's what I think. Do either of you have an idea how we can get proof on George? Smoke him out?"

Sam answered, "I do. It's something I've been thinking about. We'll need to get Henry down here so I can set it up with him or maybe Rafe can go up and see him."

"Okay, Sam, what's the idea you have?"

"I'm going to have Henry slip a sleeping powder into George's food. When he falls asleep Henry will take the bullets out of George's Colt and replace them with theatrical blanks. Then, we go up and accuse

George of killing Randy and of being George Bruell. If he's innocent, we'll be able to tell, but if he's guilty, we might be able to force him into panicking and he'll try to shoot his way out, but with blanks. We'll then have our proof."

"Okay, I like it, but where do you plan on getting these theatrical blanks?"

"They are easy to make. Pull the lead off a bullet and pack soft wax in its place. The powder stays packed and will ignite. It goes bang, but nothing comes out except a little wax. I spent some time as an actor and that's how we made our blanks for the stage."

Caden grinned. "You're a man of many surprises, Sam. Go make some blanks."

Rafe was angry over George's deception and was now convinced that he had killed Randy. He wanted to personally put the rope around his neck. He followed Sam out. "Give me the sleeping powder and blanks, I'll ride up and let Henry in on it. I'll use the excuse that Cade's not happy with his work. That will keep George from becoming suspicious."

An hour later Rafe was heading for the line shack. It was late afternoon when he arrived and George and Henry were out on the range. He tied his horse behind the corral's shed and went into the shack. Looking around inside, he took a seat and waited. An hour passed before he heard them riding in. He stepped out of the shack; both men were surprised to see him.

He walked up to Henry with an angry expression. "George, take care of the horses. Henry, Cade sent me to talk to you."

Henry's face fell. "What did I do?"

"A poor job for one thing. This is your chance to straighten up or pick up your pay. Come with me, George doesn't need to hear this."

Henry followed Rafe as he walked away from the shack. George watched them wondering what Henry could have done that was so bad he could get fired for it. He turned his back on them and led the horses to the corral.

Henry looked worried. "I thought Cade liked me, what did I do wrong?"

Rafe leaned into him. "Shut up and listen."

He explained what they had learned from Marshal Prideux. He laid out the plan and slipped Henry the sleeping powder and blanks. He left, still acting angry with him.

As he rode away, Henry walked back to the cabin with a scowl. George walked up to him. "What was that all about?"

"Oh, that damn MacMahon, can't please him sometimes. He's says I'm loafing on the job and not exercising enough security to prevent future cattle rustling. Maybe, he just needs to get up here and watch for himself."

George looked at Rafe's fading back. "Yeah, they think they're something all right. Maybe they need to lose some more cattle and then they can security that."

"Ah, the hell with them. I'm hungry, it's my turn to cook." He went in the shack and banged pans around like he was still fuming over his talk with the foreman. He put part of the powder in George's coffee and the rest in the bean juice on his plate.

An hour after eating George lay down on his bunk and fell into a deep sleep. He was still wearing his gun; however his gun side was facing out so it was a simple matter to pull the Colt and exchange the loads. He put the gun back in the holster and turned in.

In the predawn darkness Rafe, Sam, and Carl were saddled and ready to ride for the line shack. Sam came along as he was the one who realized that Randy had been shot in the back. He wanted to be there when they confronted George.

Ita came out of the house, closing the door behind her. She walked down the steps and up to the horses. She stepped into the stirrup of the horse Rafe had saddled for her. They turned at the sound of the house door closing a second time. Peering through the darkness toward the house, they saw Caden walking toward them, dressed and buckling on his gun.

Ita glared at him. "What do you think you're doing?"

"I'm riding with you. If George is a Bruell, and he killed Randy, I intend to be there. This is a personal attack on our family."

"You get back to bed; you heard what Doctor Keller said. That stuff comes apart and you die."

"I'm healed. Even where he cut me open is healed. It's been over a week and a half and I've had enough laying in bed. There's serious business that has to be taken care of and I'm sure not shoving it off on others to do. I hired him; it's my responsibility to deal with him."

Ita looked at Rafe. "What are we going to do with a kid like that?"

Rafe shrugged. "He's a MacMahon, what do you expect?"

She shook her head. "Okay, get a horse."

Rafe coughed. "Umm, Ita, he has one saddled already."

She glared at him. "What? You two cooked this up ahead of time, didn't you?"

"No, ma'am, I just know Cade."

Caden led the horse out of the corral and mounted. "Let's get this done."

The sun was up and burning off the chill of the night when the riders stopped in front of the line shack. George sat up complaining of a headache and wondering what time it was. He realized he had fallen asleep with his clothes, boots, and gun on. Henry was dressed and waiting.

George heard the horses. "What the heck is all that?" He got up and opened the door. Henry stayed behind him in the shack. He didn't want George to pull anything like locking himself in the shack and shooting his way out with real bullets.

Caden was center of the mounted group. Rafe was to his right holding his rope in his hands with a loop built. George stepped outside and glared at them, he didn't like what he saw. Even the old lady was with them and the looks he was getting were making him nervous.

His head still hurt as he looked up at Caden. "What's up with all this, Cade?"

Caden measured him with a look. "We've

come for George Bruell."

The name hit George like a face full of ice water. His eyes widened and he took a step back. Caden knew he had hit a raw nerve.

George struggled to hold his innocent expression. He shrugged. "George Bruell?"

"Are you George Bruell?"

"Not that I've ever known."

"Funny, that's not what Ed Bruell and Art Bruell said."

Once again George took the hit of ice water and he showed it. "Who are they?"

"Ed's your brother, remember? We were going to hang him but you couldn't remember if he was one of them. He kept looking right at you. That Ed Bruell."

George was shaken, but trying to hide it. He touched his dry lips with the tip of his tongue. "What did they say?"

"Ed said you were his brother, that you were part of a Natchez Under the Hill gang. That you were arrested by a marshal in the Indian Territory. That you broke jail and killed a man while escaping. That you came here to spy for Dillon Bruell in order to steal our cattle. Would you like me to go on, George?"

"What happened to Ed?"

"We hung him."

George's face fell in disbelief. He knew he

241

was trapped. His eyes shot quickly over the stone-faced group. He was aware of what the MacMahons would do if they caught him, and they had caught him, but he still had a chance.

Sam spoke up, "You probably didn't think we'd figure out that Randy was shot in the back. I looked at his body. You made a big mistake; if you had shot him in the front, we might never have put it together. There was only one man who could have shot him in the back and that was his partner who was behind him."

George jerked his Colt out, thumbed back the hammer, and pointed it at Caden. "Randy didn't leave me any choice. Now, get off that horse MacMahon, I'm riding out of here."

Caden remained as he was, calmly looking at him. "In Randy's note he was trying to say George *shot* me, he wasn't trying to spell saddle. That was my mistake. I trusted you, but we'll remedy that."

"I'll blow you out of that saddle and everyone else who tries to stop me. Now, get down."

Caden continued to stare at him. "You came here to scout us out for the rest of the Bruell gang, didn't you?"

George sneered, "You're so smart, you

figure it out."

"Looks like we already have."

The sneer on George's face turned to a sarcastic grin. "You do know that it was Art who dry-gulched you, right? Did he tell you that? I had told him to keep his mouth shut 'cause he always talked too much. I told him not to rile up the mighty MacMahons. When I found out he had shot you, I beat the hell out of him. He always was a bragger and too stupid to live. I told Dillon way back in Natchez we needed to kill him, but, oh no, not his baby brother. I suppose this is his way of getting even. Now, get off that horse, MacMahon."

"No."

Still pointing the gun at Caden, George pulled the trigger. The gun boomed and Caden remained in the saddle. George stared at him in shock. He thumbed back the hammer and fired again with the same results. He fired a third time. "What the hell?"

Rafe spun the lariat once dropping the loop over George's head. Jerking the slack out of the rope, Rafe closed the loop around his upper arms. George immediately began to struggle. Henry jumped on him from the back and pummeled his head with his fists as they fell. "You killed Randy, damn you!

You killed my pal!"

Caden shouted, "Henry, get him on his feet."

Staggering from the punches Henry had delivered, George was led to an oak tree with a protruding branch. Carl led George's haltered horse and stopped him under the tree. He and Henry shoved George up on the bareback horse while Rafe cinched the loop around George's neck and flung the remainder of the rope over the branch and then back over it a second time. He pulled George's head up hard and dallied the end of the rope several turns around his saddle-horn and turned his horse sideways to the branch.

George's expression was a mix of fear and hate. He glared at the faces that glared back at him. "Why didn't my gun work?"

Henry looked at him. "I filled it with blanks while you took your beauty sleep."

He glared at Henry. "Traitor."

"Oh, that's rich; you have a lot of room to talk. I ride for the MacMahon brand, that's where my loyalties lie, not with the likes of you."

The look George gave Caden was full of hate. "Is this how you hung my brother? Ganged up on him like this?"

"We've never seen your brother. Come to

think of it, we haven't seen Art either."

"What?"

Caden gestured toward Henry who un-hooked the lead rope off the halter and slapped it across the horse's rump. The horse bolted and the rope snapped hard against the branch and Rafe's saddlehorn. They watched the body swing on the rope until the momentum ceased and the outlaw hung loose and lifeless. Rafe released the rope and George's body dropped to the ground.

Ita looked at the body and then at Rafe. "Drag him out of here and let the coyotes and buzzards have him. I don't want him buried in the same earth Randy's in." Rafe grabbed the loose end of the rope, dallied it around the horn, and moved his horse forward dragging the body behind him.

Carl looked at Henry. "I'm your new partner. Cade assigned me with you."

"Good, I'd like to work with a man I can trust."

Caden, Ita, and Sam turned back solemnly for home. It wasn't a pleasant thing they did, but a necessary one. You didn't steal MacMahon cattle, you didn't murder their people, and you never betrayed MacMahon trust.

CHAPTER FOURTEEN

The morning after the shooting in the Crystal Queen, Miles and Bren found Stanford's ranch. They rode through the cattle, looking them over. Bren glanced at Miles, "Bar Lazy 8 M? What kind of a brand is that?"

"A busy one. Probably meant to cover other brands." He looked up. "We've got company."

Bren looked up to see two riders approaching. They stopped and waited. The men pulled their horses up in front of them. The older of the two gave them a scrutinizing look-over. "You men are trespassing,"

Miles' expression was calm. "We're just passing through."

The younger of the two men had the look of a trouble hunter. He bobbed his head in a cocky manner and screwed his lip up when he spoke. "The man just said you were trespassing. Seems like you ought to at least apologize and beg off so we don't hurt you."

Miles eyed him steady and cold. "Figure you're man enough? You might be biting off enough to choke to death on."

The older man knew a fight was coming. It wasn't the first time the kid had picked a fight when there didn't need to be one. He cut it off. "You men can just ride on."

Miles kept his eyes on the kid while addressing the older man. "Whose land are we on anyway?"

"Dillon Stanford's."

"Dillon Stanford of Stanfordville?"

"That's the one."

Bren asked him, "Is that Stanford's brand on those cows?"

The kid spoke again, "Yeah, the Bar Lazy 8 M. If you see it again, you'd better turn back."

"And if we don't?" Bren locked eyes with the kid.

The kid didn't know what to say. He wanted to show how tough he was, but didn't expect to get called on his threat. He had talked himself into a corner he had no idea how to get out of.

"That's what I thought, all mouth." Bren moved his horse forward, keeping his eyes on the kid as he passed him. Miles followed, turning in the saddle to watch the men behind them. The two riders stayed in place for several seconds and then rode on.

Miles spoke without looking at Bren, "Okay, we've got his ranch and his brand. The buffalo hunter said folks went to Curlew or Logan Valley for supplies. Let's head up to Curlew and see what the people there have to say about Stanfordville and Dillon's gang."

They rode north until they came into Curlew. The atmosphere of the town was drastically different from that of Stanford-ville. Women walked freely about, children played in a yard next to a schoolhouse, and wagons were parked alongside the stores while men loaded supplies into them. Nowhere were there outlaws loafing around.

Stopping in front of a saloon, they dismounted and went inside. It was an average saloon for the country, a bar and a few tables. A couple of men were at the bar and others were talking around a bottle at a table. It wasn't a busy place. The barkeep was behind the bar wiping it clean.

They stepped up to the bar. The barkeep smiled at them. "How are you two today?"

Miles smiled back. "We're just fine. How about a couple of whiskeys."

"Got it." He placed the glasses down and

filled them. "Passing through?"

"Yeah. We stopped at that, what was it Bren? Stanfordville?"

Bren nodded. "Yeah, Stanfordville." He looked at the barkeep. "Talk about an unfriendly town." He whistled to accentuate his comment.

"Oh, yeah, stay away from there. That Dillon Stanford is a mean man and he keeps a lot of toughs around to make sure things are run his way."

Bren looked at him. "His way?"

The man nodded. "He owns every business in that town. He built it up several years back and a lot of people borrowed money from him or paid him to start in business. He holds the notes on the loans. On the businesses he doesn't control, he demands protection payments from them or his thugs cause trouble. I feel sorry for those people. They're trapped in that town. No one around here buys there, they mostly come here."

Miles shook his head. "Sounds pretty rough for those people stuck in there. Why don't they leave?"

"Some have tried, but they end up dead before they get far out of town. That puts the fear into the rest of them."

"Must be a pretty bad man, this Dillon

Stanford. Know where he comes from?"

"Him and his wife came from up north somewhere, nine, ten years ago. I was working here and people were talking about him building up a ranch and then a town. Stanford bought his supplies here until they got set up. They were pretty secretive about what they were doing and didn't talk much to anyone, which of course gave rise to a lot of rumors. Some said they were on the run from the law. There was one story that claimed they had committed a couple of murders out on their place."

"Murders?"

"Some kid said he saw Stanford and his wife murder two men and bury them. He was just a kid; they have wild imaginations, so no one paid him much mind."

"Did they murder two men?"

The man shrugged. "Who knows. When people stay to themselves, all kinds of rumors get started. Of course, seeing what that place has turned into and what the Stanfords are like now, maybe that kid wasn't wrong."

"We hear tell that there's an outlaw gang running wild around these parts."

"You heard right. There's been a lot of stock rustling; stages held up, travelers robbed. Once again rumor says that it's Dillon Stanford and his thugs that are the gang. That's what people around here think anyway."

"What do you think?"

"I think they're right."

Miles and Bren finished their drinks and left. Miles looked up and down the street. "Let's talk to people and see if we can't narrow down the outlaws' pattern."

Bren stepped into the saddle. "I don't know about you, but I could use something to eat. I saw a sign down this way that said something about a café."

"Lead on."

They rode down the street toward the café sign. Beyond the café and past the last store was a large square building with a rail running around it. Green cowhides were hung over the railing. "Looks like a tanner," Bren commented to Miles.

A big black skin draped over a rail caught Bren's eye and peaked his curiosity. "Let's go up there and see if he knows anything about Stanford's brand. If anyone does, it would be a tanner." They rode past the café and on to the tanner's barn.

Bren stopped and looked at the black hide. It had the Bar Lazy 8 M on it. He pointed at it. "That's a horsehide and it's got Stanford's brand on it. You said it could be a cover for something, let's have a look."

They dismounted for a closer look. As they walked toward the black horsehide a man in a leather apron came out of the building. "Morning, help you with something?"

Bren pointed at the horsehide. "I was curious about that brand."

"Oh, that's Dillon Stanford's brand. I have a deal with his foreman to get all the hides from any cattle they butcher or that die on his place."

"But, that's a horsehide."

"Yes it is, and lucky for me. I don't get a lot of horsehides, mostly all cattle, but I have a good market for horsehide blacksmiths aprons. That one there was from one of Stanford's Morgans that died. It was an old horse and just dropped dead."

"He raises Morgans?"

"And some nice ones too. He came in with several head of brood stock and built them up on his ranch. He has the only Morgan herd in this part of the country and people pay top dollar for them. They're a great horse for pulling wagons and look good in front of a buggy."

Bren stared at the hide for a moment and then walked up to it while Miles continued to talk with the tanner. He ran his hand over the brand and then flipped the soft green hide over. He stood in shock staring at the hide. "Miles, come here."

Miles moved away from the tanner. "What?"

Bren pointed at the underside of the hide. Miles swore under his breath. The underside of the brand revealed an OM. He traced the old brand scar with his finger.

"Pa would have branded those horses before he left Minnesota with them."

Miles was momentarily stunned. "He sure would have. Owen was no fool; he branded everything and it only stands to reason he would brand those Morgans he bought."

The tanner walked up to them. "Is there a problem?"

Bren flipped the hide back over so the hair side was up showing Stanford's brand.

Miles asked him, "How good of friends are you with Dillon Stanford?"

"We're not, I can't stand the man. That's why I deal with his ranch foreman. Why?"

Miles pointed at the Bar Lazy 8 M, and then flipped the hide over to show the OM, and then flipped it back. He never said a word; he just flipped the hide again showing the underside and the OM while watching the tanner's expression.

The tanner's face showed genuine shock.

He took the hide from Bren's hand and flipped it back hair side out and looked at the ∞M that made the Lazy 8 M. "That brand was altered. The original brand can always be seen on the underside of the hide. I never looked at it. Didn't have any reason to." He flipped the hide back and forth several times looking closely at the two brands.

Miles said dryly, "That's right. The left-hand circle of the Lazy 8 snugs right up against the O of OM."

"So, who has the OM brand?"

"We do," Bren broke in. "It's the Mac-Mahon brand."

"I've heard of the MacMahons. Up Niobrara way?"

Bren nodded. "That's us. Eight years ago my pa and brother were coming back from Minnesota with seven Morgans to build a herd. He had a chestnut stud, three black and three bay mares with him. He never made it home."

Bren looked at Miles whose face was turning dark and angry. "I think we just found out what happened to them."

The tanner looked shaken. "I swear, I didn't know. I had nothing to do with this."

"We know that," Bren assured him. "But, we know now that Dillon Stanford did."

"This was one of the older black mares. I've seen his horses a few times and he does have an older chestnut stud. Some bay and black mares too."

Bren frowned. "I'll bet he does. I want that section of hide with the brand on it. How much do you want for it?"

The tanner pulled a knife from his belt and cut out a large section of the hide with the altered brand in the center of it. He handed it to Bren. "Take it."

"You're losing money on it, let me pay you."

The man shook his head. "Use it for proof. Show it to the law. It's the least I can do for you, seeing what happened. If you can bring down Dillon Stanford, you will be doing the whole country a service. And, if you need me to tell the law what I know, I'll be glad to."

Bren put out his hand. "Thank you. I won't forget this. A favor done for a Mac-Mahon is never forgotten."

The tanner took his hand. "Ryan Smith."

"Bren, and this is my uncle, Miles." Miles shook his hand.

Bren looked at him. "Thanks again. Every cowhide that comes off the MacMahon ranch will come to you from here on. I hope you can turn a few dollars on them."

"Why, thank you. The more hides I get the more I can make, and sometimes they're in short supply."

Bren looked at Miles. "That story about the kid seeing Stanford kill two men wasn't just a tale." He rolled the piece of hide and tied it behind his saddle. "Let's go to Stanfordville."

"I want to get a look at those Morgans on Stanford's ranch first. We'll pose as horse buyers; I need to see the brands on the rest of those horses. I want a close look; we should be able to tell if our brand was added onto." Mounting up they turned back toward Dillon Stanford's ranch.

They arrived at the ranch late in the day. There was no owner's house, as Stanford lived in town. The foreman's house was the first structure they came to. They rode up to it, dismounted, and knocked on his door. The foreman came to the door and Miles explained that they were interested in buying a couple of the Morgans. The foreman was quick to take them out to the small fenced pasture where the horses were kept separate from the cattle.

They acted as if each horse was one they were interested in. They were of varying ages, but they all carried the Stanford brand. Taking their time to look through the horses, they came back to the barn where other horses were stabled. The foreman explained that these were the older horses; a few were the original brood stock for the herd.

Miles and Bren looked them over. There were four mares, two blacks, two bays, and the chestnut stud. They pretended to be studying the horses while actually giving a close look at the brands. On close examination it could be seen where the left circle of the ∞ of the Lazy 8 had been added to the O. On two of them there was actually a tiny gap between the two halves of the 8 where the cinch ring that had been used to alter the brand had not lined up close enough. There was also a slight difference in the sizes of the two circles, which would not happen if the brand was a one-piece construction. It was proof enough that these had been the horses Owen and Aiden had been bringing home before being murdered by Dillon Stanford and Kelly.

They left, telling the foreman that they would have to think about the purchase. They left the ranch headed for the Crystal Queen. They were going to call it to Dillon's face and let the chips fall where they may.

Arriving at the Crystal Queen, Miles and

Bren stormed in through the door. The saloon was busy with the roulette wheel spinning, men playing cards, and everyone drinking. Men turned their attention toward them. Outlaws, as well as those not associated with them, were in the room; some recognized them from the fight and shooting the day before.

Miles was slightly ahead of Bren as they walked swiftly toward the closed door. Two men stood up in front of them to block their path. Miles never missed a step as he grabbed the back of an empty chair and slammed it into the first man he encountered. Bren followed suit, taking the second man down with a chair.

Miles reared back his booted and spurred foot and drove the heel into the door, sending it flying open. The door smashed hard against the inside wall as pieces of door frame and doorknob blasted across the room. Dillon was sitting behind a desk while Kelly and Art sat to either side. They jumped to their feet, startled by the crashing door.

Miles grabbed Dillon by the front of his shirt and yanked him over the desk, dragging everything on top of it with him. Papers and glasses hit the floor in a flurry of crashes. Art came at them only to be met with Bren's right fist in his face. He hit the floor hard.

Kelly pulled a gun from a pocket in her dress. Bren slapped down on her hand, sending the small revolver spinning across the floor. He pulled his Colt and told her and Art to get their hands in the air and move back against the wall. Still sitting on the floor Art slid toward the wall until his back was against it. Kelly moved back next to Art and glared her hate at Bren.

Miles snarled in Dillon's face. "You murdered my brother."

Dillon knew Miles MacMahon; he also knew how dangerous he was. He had been hiding ever since his thugs had brought him the message that Miles was looking for him. He wheezed through the choking collar Miles had twisted in his hands. "You're crazy, MacMahon, I never murdered anyone."

"Bar Lazy 8 M over the OM. We found it on the Morgans you killed him for."

Dillon Stanford's face was turning purple and he was gasping for air. Kelly and Art looked on, not wanting to challenge Bren's .45. The room was suddenly rushed by several men who pointed guns at Miles and Bren. Bren kept his gun pointed at Kelly's head. They had a standoff.

Miles looked at them and cursed. He let go of Dillon's collar. Dillon lay on the floor gasping, his eyes wild with fear. Miles pulled his gun and faced those of Stanford's thugs. "A lot of lead will get thrown real fast here, boys. Who wants to die first? My partner will not hesitate to blow Kelly's head off." He could see the hesitation in their eyes. These were sure-thing killers and they knew some of them would die and they didn't care for the odds.

Dillon waved at his men. "Let them go, just get them out of here." The outlaws holstered their guns.

Miles looked down at Dillon, who was still on the floor. "We're not done here, not by a damn sight." He held the gun on the men.

Bren switched his gun from Kelly to the outlaws. They eased out of the room each facing in opposite directions and covering the area to their right and left. No one moved from their seats or from the bar. Some of them had seen what happened the last time these two were in the room. Miles and Bren backed out the door.

Pulling the reins loose from the hitch rail, guns still out and ready, they stood between the horses, looking around them before they mounted. A man walked out of the saloon and headed toward them. Miles laid his arm

260

over the saddle, leveling his gun on him. He could see the man was a couple of years younger than Bren and he was wearing the outfit of a working cowboy.

Miles snapped at him, "What do you want?"

The young cowboy held his hands out in front of him. "Easy. I overheard what you said in there about Stanford murdering your brother and about the Morgan horses."

"What about it?"

"My name is Luke Swenson. When I was a kid, I saw him and her murder two men and steal their horses. There were seven good Morgans and they took them, and robbed their bodies too. I was a kid then and no one would believe me. I can show you where the bodies are buried."

CHAPTER FIFTEEN

Luke Swenson left town with Miles and Bren. He told them that he had been working for a rancher to the east, but the rancher was a tyrant to the men, working them to death and then coming up short on wages at the end of the month. He had quit and now had free time on his hands.

He led them back toward the Stanford ranch. He told them the story as he had witnessed it. "When I was a kid, I used to hunt the country that Stanford's ranch is now on. My pa was dead and I hunted for us to eat. I had seen this man and a woman move in and build a cabin on the place. It was a poor cabin; the man had no building skill.

"I kept away from them when I passed through. There was something about them that scared me. Then, one day I was out there and the two of them come in trailing these real nice horses. Well, they sure didn't seem to have any money to buy good stock like that with, but they had 'em. I hid in the brush and watched.

"They were acting nervous and scared. I heard them talking about hiding the horses because someone was hot on their tail. They talked some more, and then left the horses tied right out in the middle of a clearing. It wasn't far from their cabin and the horses could be seen for a long ways. Them two disappeared and I thought it pretty queer that they had done that.

"Pretty soon two riders come up the same trail. One was older than the other, and they looked plum put out, and they were a real skookum pair, real tough looking, you know. They come up on the horses and I heard them talking about finding their horses. Then all hell broke loose with shooting. That man and woman bushwhacked those two men and shot 'em to pieces. They run out, both carrying rifles, and looked at those two men on the ground. They looked sure enough dead, but he put a bullet in each of their heads anyway.

"Well, that man and woman went to searching the bodies and pulling stuff out of their pockets. I tell you what, I was plum scared. I just laid down in that brush flatter'n any injun ever did and watched. I figured if they knew I was there they'd shoot me sure as anything. Well, the man he rips open the older man's shirt and strips a money belt off of him. He opened it and it was chalk full of greenbacks. He yelled at the woman to come see and they went to yahooing all over the place.

"He stuffed the money in his pockets. He found some papers that they read and got to acting all scared again. I heard them saying something about Mac-somebody and miles or something. They cleaned out the saddlebags and then put all the tack on a pile. They stripped the dead men plum naked and put the clothes on the tack. He takes off and comes back pretty quick with a fuel can and a shovel. They piled dead brush on the tack and clothes, doused it with fuel from the can, and then lit it up. It was a big fire.

"They dug a couple of shallow graves and buried the bodies. They piled rocks on 'em and some cut brush. They stuck around until everything was burned and then shoveled dirt over it all. I know now it was Dillon Stanford and his woman, but I didn't then. I told some folks in Curlew and around, but they told me to stop making up stories. My ma told me to be quiet about it before they came and killed all of us.

"Right after that is when they brought in cattle and built up the town. They didn't have anything until they robbed those men and then they were flush with money. Now, Stanford has all those Morgans he's so famous for and they all came from those horses he stole and killed those men for."

Miles and Bren rode in silence, taking in the story. Bren looked at Luke. "That was my pa and brother. They went to Minnesota to buy those horses and they never came back. We never knew what happened to them."

Luke nodded. "Sorry about your folks. That's what happened, though."

"Thanks, Luke, for telling us." Bren reached his hand out to him. "I'm Bren MacMahon." They shook hands. "That's Miles, my uncle. He's probably the one they were talking about, Dillon knew Miles from the Army. Miles sent him to prison at one time. That was probably the bill of sale on the horses they saw and got scared at the name."

Luke looked surprised. "MacMahon. The Niobrara MacMahons?"

"That's right."

"I've heard some stories about you folks. It's said to be safer to snuggle up to a grizzly bear than cross a MacMahon. Guess

265

Stanford's cut his throat now."

"I guess he has."

They skirted around the Stanford property to the far northern end. Luke led them down a draw to a grassy flat interspersed with clumps of head-high brush. An abandoned cabin with a collapsing roof stood on one end of the flat. Luke pointed to a spot overgrown with tall grass and half surrounded by brush. "Right there is where they're buried." He then pointed to a spot covered in sparse grass twenty feet away. "And there's where they burned everything."

They dismounted and Bren ripped the grass out of the spot where Luke said the graves were. He dug out several large rocks that eight years of blowing sand had covered. He poked his knife into the ground and started to dig.

Luke stood over him and watched. "They were buried shallow, so you shouldn't have to dig deep."

Miles stood next to Luke watching intently. Bren had dug down only a foot when he struck something solid. He worked the knife under it and flipped up a bone. He dug around and found several more, and then a skull with a bullet hole in it. He looked up at Miles and they exchanged a silent agreement that this was the remains of either Owen or Aiden.

The confirmation that it was Owen came when Luke pointed to the graves. "That was the older man. The younger one should be to the right of him."

Bren left the graves and began to dig in the spot where the fire had been. He found buckles and saddle rings. He dug out some more and came to an iron rod. He pulled it up; it was rusted and dirt caked, but the OM on the end of the branding iron completed the story.

He looked up at Miles as a shot rang out and spit dirt up in his face. They dove into the surrounding brush as several more shots rang out and echoed off the draws and hills. They had no idea where the shots were coming from. They lay still watching and listening for movement, but saw nothing. At least a dozen shots were fired into the brush where they lay before the shooting stopped. Then, in the distance they could hear a horse running.

Miles got up and cursed. "Ten to one that was Dillon. Come on, we can get him in his town."

Luke asked excitedly, "Can I come?"

"Come on, let's go." Bren waved to him.

They jumped on their horses and put

them into a gallop for Stanfordville. The town was not far from the ranch, as Dillon had built it up on his original piece of land and expanded the ranch from there. The ride was a short one. Miles figured Dillon kept his horse at the livery so that was where he was likely headed. He told Bren to go to the saloon and head him off there if he missed him at the livery.

Galloping down the back street, Miles slid his horse to a stop in front of the big barn. He jumped off and ran for the open double doors of the livery. The churned-up tracks of a hard-ridden horse went in through the doors. He pulled his Colt and slipped a sixth cartridge into the cylinder that he usually kept empty under the hammer and then held the gun down at his side. He walked in cautiously looking around. A winded, sweat-covered horse was standing inside. He heard a man running and turned to see Dillon Stanford trying to escape out the rear door.

Miles brought the Colt up, aimed it at him, and shouted across the open space of the barn. "Hold it right there, Stanford."

Stanford turned toward him. Seeing the gun pointed at him, he stopped. He was breathing hard. "What do you want with me, MacMahon? Why don't you leave me alone? Didn't you do enough already? I got five years in prison for what you done."

"You were caught in the act of robbing the bodies of your own fellow soldiers. It was my pleasure to speak against you at the court-martial. You're horse manure, Stanford, and you got off lucky, if I could have put you in front of a firing squad, I would have."

"Go to hell, MacMahon."

"You also said that you would kill me if you ever saw me again. You just tried and failed, but it's what I would have expected from you, to shoot from ambush, shoot in the back. You're a murdering coward, Stanford."

Dillon only stood and stared at him.

Miles closed the distance between them, the muzzle of the Colt held steady on Stanford. "We saw the horses with the altered brands. We found the bodies you buried. You murdered my brother and nephew and then built your little empire here on the money you stole from their dead bodies."

"Pure supposition, you have no proof."

"I have an eyewitness."

"I doubt it. You're trying to make something out of nothing."

"I know enough. I've seen and heard enough to know you and Kelly murdered them and then burned everything. Only thing is branding irons don't burn and you left a branding iron when you burned the rigs. Knowing Owen, he had it tucked up under the saddle skirt and in your rush to burn everything, you missed it."

"It's all lies, MacMahon. You can't have me arrested on lies and suspicion."

Suddenly feeling confident that Mac-Mahon had nothing he could hold against him, he grew bolder. "Besides, even if I did kill them, it's been too long to bring it to trial. You could never prove it was me. You couldn't even prove it was them in the graves; it's just a bunch of bones that could belong to anybody. You'd never get a conviction."

Dillon was growing more confident by the second. He knew he had his old enemy beat. He laughed out loud, "I'm a big man around here and I own everyone in town. You could never find a jury of twelve men to convict me, even if you could get me to trial. All I have to do is keep denying everything and walk away a free man and you know it." His face broke into a triumphant smirk. "You might as well give up MacMahon. You can't prove a thing."

Stanford continued to sport the "I beat you" smile as Miles moved to within six feet of him, the gun still up, the hammer cocked back. "I don't intend to bring you to trial, Stanford. I don't need to prove who is in the graves, I know who it is, and I know who put them there. I don't need twelve jurors to convict you."

Dillon laughed. "What are you going to do, shoot me? I'm unarmed."

"I don't give a damn if you're armed or not."

The smile began to fade as worry grew in Dillon's eyes. "You can't just shoot me."

"Sure I can. It's what we call the jury of six. Six .45 slugs. It's a jury that always returns a guilty verdict. You and I both know what you did and you're not walking out of here laughing about it."

Dillon's voice, filled with fear, came out in a high pitch, "You can't just shoot me."

"Six jurors, Dillon." He pulled the trigger. The bullet smacked into Dillon Stanford's chest. His face twisted in horror and pain. "One. Guilty."

Miles shot him again. "Two. Guilty."

He shot four more times as fast as he could cock the hammer and pull the trigger. After each shot he repeated the word, "guilty." He looked down at Dillon Stanford's lifeless body, the shocked look still on his face. "Jury of six, Dillon. They find you guilty as charged."

As Miles looked down at Dillon's body a rifle landed hard on the ground next to it. Miles' head jerked up to see the hostler standing in front of him. "It's his from off his saddle, I saw him try to shoot you with that rifle. Looks like you beat him, though."

Miles looked at him calmly. "Looks that way, don't it."

Miles dumped the empty brass shells from the Colt and thumbed in new cartridges as he turned and walked out of the barn. People were gathering. He heard the hostler come out and announce that Dillon Stanford was dead. A cheer went up from the crowd. It would only be a matter of minutes before the word was all across town.

Stepping back into his saddle, Miles rode toward the Crystal Queen. Bren and Luke were coming toward him from the street in front of the saloon. Bren shouted out, "We heard shooting."

"Dillon's dead. Let's go in and root out Art and Kelly." The three men walked into the saloon. Miles called out, "You men are out of work, your boss is dead." The room went silent.

He kicked open the broken office door to find Art and Kelly standing as if expecting someone. They jumped at the slamming door; their faces fell upon seeing him.

"Expecting someone else? Dillon's dead."

Before Miles could say anything else, he heard a shuffle of boots on the wooden floor behind him. He turned to see two men. "Get back," he snarled at them.

One of the men spoke in a hard voice, "Are you Miles MacMahon?"

"That's me."

"I'm U.S. Marshal Prideux out of Yankton, and this is Marshal Wills out of Omaha. We're here to arrest Dillon, Art, George, and Ed Bruell. Caden told me you were here."

Miles stared at him for a second before finding his voice. "Who are the Bruells?"

"Their names are Bruell, not Stanford. They're the leaders of a criminal gang from Mississippi. I'll explain it later. Where are they?"

"We haven't seen anything of George or Ed. Dillon is dead." He pointed at Art. "This is Art." He pointed at Kelly. "You can add her to your list too. Kelly, whatever her last name is these days. She's Dillon's wife, or woman, or whatever."

Prideux looked at her and Art. Both were showing fear and panic. Kelly burst out, "It wasn't me. Dillon and Art ran the gang."

Art snarled at her. "Shut up."

Kelly's voice grew in volume as she panicked, "Dillon killed the two MacMahon men with the horses. It wasn't me." She pointed at Art. "It was him, he's the one who wired Dillon and told him that two men were coming with Morgan horses. He said we should take the horses when they got to Yankton."

He screamed in her face, "Shut up, you stupid woman!"

"We took them, but he set it up, he's just as guilty. He killed that other MacMahon too, he said so."

Without warning Art pulled a pistol out of his pocket. He screamed in growing hysterics, "Shut up!" He pointed the gun and shot her.

She shrieked and fell to the floor. Prideux jerked out his pistol and shot Art in the head. The black powder smoke floated in the air with a bitter smell. The room was suddenly quiet as they looked at the bodies on the floor. Prideux turned to Miles. "That was a hell of a thing."

Prideux shook his head. With the gun still in his hand, he spun and marched hard-heeled out of the office. The saloon was silent, as all in it had heard the exchange of shouts and gunfire through the open office door. In a booming voice, Prideux announced to the room, "I am U.S. Marshal

Prideux, and I am accompanied by Marshal Wills. Any man who is not a resident of this town, a business owner, or gainfully employed has one hour to leave town. If you are still here in one hour, you will be either arrested or shot."

A man with the look of an outlaw to him jumped up out of his chair. "Stanford owes me money."

"For what? Stealing cattle? Go ahead and say yes and we will be happy to take you down to the livery barn and hang you from the hay boom."

The man grumbled, shoved his chair, and walked out. Several men followed him across the floor as the exodus of outlaws filed out the door to the tune of curses and complaints.

CHAPTER SIXTEEN

Within minutes of Prideux's announcement, the Crystal Queen was empty except
for the barkeep. The legitimate residents of
the town left to spread the word of the
events. A sense of excitement was on them
as they raced out to tell their friends that
the whole Stanford outfit was dead and
their thugs were fleeing before the marshals.

Miles looked across the room at the
barkeep. The man gave him a smile and
tapped his fingers to his forehead in a quick
salute. He was pleased and it showed.

Bren and Luke were standing by the door
watching the men file out, making sure
there were no attempts to shoot and run.
Prideux looked at Wills. "That was fast."
Wills' face remained stern as he nodded in
agreement.

Prideux waved Bren and Luke over to
him. He pulled out a chair and cast a glance
at the men around him. "Sit down, gentle-

men; I want to know what went on prior to that little show in the office." They all pulled up chairs and sat around in a circle.

The barkeep brought a bottle and a fistful of glasses. He set them on the table. "Compliments of the house, gentlemen." He turned and walked away.

They each poured a drink.

"Okay," Prideux began, "I've been to your house and was filled in on the past events that you were involved in. The rustling, the murdered hired man, and so on. Mrs. Stanford told me about their move from Minnesota to Nebraska and how her husband had changed. She didn't know he had a criminal past and that his real name was Bruell." He looked at Miles. "What do you know about Dillon Bruell?"

"I've only known him as Dillon Stanford. I was a civilian scout for the Army during the Sioux campaigns of the '60's. Dillon came into the company about '63. He was a coward and a sneak; it was obvious right from the start. A year after he had signed on, we had a running battle with the Sioux. We managed to drive them off and had returned to pick up our dead. That's when I caught him stealing money from the pockets of the dead soldiers. I turned him over to the commander. He was arrested. I spoke against him at the trial; he was court martialed, and sent to prison.

"When he got out, he hung around Yankton gambling and in general being the scum he was. I was still with the Army and stationed at Fort Randall. I saw him around whenever I went into Yankton. He took to hanging with a prostitute named Kelly." He pointed toward the office. "She changed her name to Maude, but that's her lying in there.

"Then one day they both disappeared. The word around was that he had won a piece of land in a poker game and left. I never heard from him again until Cade started seeing Jo Stanford and Dillon's name came up again as being the brother of her father. That would be Art, who you done in back there."

Prideux listened intently and then asked, "Why did you decide to come here looking for him?"

"Because we got fed up with the rustling and shootings that were spawned from him. After talking to a couple of our rancher neighbors, it was obvious we had a gang of outlaws creating havoc in the area. I suspected this Dillon here and the one I knew were one in the same. Bren and I came here to put an end to the thieving and murders."

For the first time Wills spoke up. "You took the law into your own hands then?"

The comment irritated Miles. He looked at the lawman. "I didn't see any badges around when Randy was killed. I guess I missed the deputies and sheriff's posse when we hunted the group down and shot it out with them. If we wanted this outlaw business stopped it was up to us to stop it, just like we've done for the last twenty-five years we've been here."

Wills looked at Miles with his hard gray eyes. He didn't like Miles' answer.

Prideux glanced at his fellow officer. "MacMahon here was a marshal in Wichita and North Platte. He's also right; the law is spread thin up here. Down your way it's different. Up here we need the help."

Miles studied Marshal Wills; he was a tough man, the kind of man the country needed. "We don't have to be at odds, Marshal Wills. It's a hard country that requires hard men to make hard decisions."

Wills' eyes relaxed. "No, we don't. You being a former lawman makes some difference."

Miles turned his attention back to Prideux. "Back about eight years ago, my brother, Owen, and his eldest son went to Mankato to buy Morgan brood stock to

279

breed them on the ranch. Owen sent a letter to Ita from Mankato describing the horses and that they were headed back. In Sioux Falls he sent another saying they had made it that far and would contact her again upon reaching Yankton. No one heard from them again. We searched for months and never came up with so much as a clue to their disappearance."

While Miles told the story, Bren left the room and returned with the piece of rolled-up horsehide. Miles had stopped talking so Bren began. "Our brand is the OM; Stanford's, or I guess you can now say Bruell's, is a Bar Lazy 8 M."

Bren unrolled the horsehide with the hair side out. "We were riding past a tanner's building in Curlew when I spotted this horsehide hanging over a rail. I saw this Stanford brand on it. The tanner said it was from one of Stanford's older Morgans that had died. That just kind of rang a bell in my head. I looked hard at the brand and it looked wrong. My pa would have branded those horses before he set out with them. I flipped the hide over and found this."

He turned the hide around so the flesh side faced the marshals. The lawmen both stared at the perfect reversed OM on the underside. "We knew then that Dillon Stanford had a hand in their disappearance. We went to his ranch to look at the other Morgan horses and he had five older horses that matched the description my pa had sent us about the horses he had bought. We took a close look at the brands and could see ours had been added to. The left circle of the Lazy 8 didn't fit right up against the O, they had been sloppy about it."

Miles added to the story. "Owen had just sold a herd in Omaha and had several thousand dollars on him in a money belt. As we later learned, Dillon and Kelly suddenly became rich about that same time."

Miles gestured toward Luke. "Then we met Luke and he had a very interesting story to tell us. Go ahead Luke and tell them what you told us."

The marshals turned their attention to the young cowboy as he related the murder of the two men and the burning of their property. He told it exactly as he had to Miles and Bren, describing the events in detail and confirming that the people he saw turned out to be Dillon Stanford and Kelly, who called herself Maude.

When he finished, Miles continued, "Luke took us out to the place and Bren started digging around and found the graves. He also dug in the spot where their saddles and outfits had been burned. He found one of our branding irons that had been with the outfit that Dillon missed in his hurry to cover up his crime. That's when someone started shooting at us. We heard a horse running off and we followed it. I caught up with the shooter at the livery barn, it was Dillon."

Prideux listened without comment to the stories from the three men. He asked, "You said Dillon was dead?"

"I shot him."

Prideux nodded. "Sounds like a reasonable course of action under the circumstances." He looked at Wills as if seeking agreement.

Wills looked back at him. "A man has a right to defend himself."

Miles looked at them for a moment and then added, "I think you can see this was an outlaw town. Folks here are, or were, scared of the Stanfords and their outlaws. The people living around here do their buying anywhere but here. Stanford built this town and his ranch with the money he stole from my brother. He then ruled it like a feudal tyrant with threats and extorting money from the businessmen for protection. I understand that those who tried to leave disappeared, probably murdered."

When Miles finished talking, Marshal Wills stood up. "I'd like to see these horses and the graves. Graves first. How about you, Prideux?"

"Yes, I would. We will need to seize all of Bruell's holdings until we can sort it out, but I want to see the evidence first."

The men got up from the table as the undertaker was coming in. He stopped in front of the men with the badges. "I'm here for the bodies."

Prideux jerked his thumb toward the office with the open door where the bodies of Kelly and Art lay sprawled on the floor. "In there."

"Umm, say Marshal, who is going to pay for the funerals?"

"Funerals? There won't be any funerals. Just dig a hole and stick them in it, same hole as far as I'm concerned."

The man frowned. "Hardly worth my time."

"Well, undertaker, that's not my problem, but if you find a couple bucks in Art's pockets, you can keep it for your trouble."

The man nodded and walked into the office as the marshals left the saloon with Miles, Bren, and Luke. The undertaker had a wagon parked in front of the saloon. In the back was the body of Dillon Bruell. Prideux looked at it and then at Miles. "I take it that's Dillon."

"That's him."

"He's a mess, how many times did you shoot him?"

Miles shrugged. "Enough."

Prideux grinned as they walked away. He had no sympathy for animals like Dillon Bruell. Pulling their horses loose, they mounted and rode for the Stanford ranch. As they left town, several businessmen came out to the boardwalk smiling and waving as they passed. Miles leaned toward Bren, "I think we made a lot of people happy."

As they rode, Prideux told them what he had learned about the Bruells and their criminal activities on the Natchez Trace. How they had split up with Art going to Minnesota and assuming a new name, which he and Dillon must have agreed on as they both took Stanford. He was sorry for Anna Stanford, that she had been deceived through twenty years of marriage. Dillon enlisted in the Army no doubt figuring it was a good place to hide.

Wills had heard this before so his mind was thinking ahead. "That still leaves their cousins, George and Ed. Do you know anything in regards to them? Any idea at all?"

Prideux shook his head. "None at all if they aren't in this town. My guess would be they broke with their cousins and moved someplace away from them."

Luke led them to the place on Stanford's ranch where he had been earlier with Bren and Miles. The churned-up dirt from Bren's digging had not been disturbed. All was as they left it when Dillon began shooting at them and they gave chase. The marshals looked the area over from the higher position offered on horseback.

They dismounted and were followed by the others. Luke pointed and explained further what he had witnessed, showing them the exact location of each detail of the crime. Wills studied the grave Bren had churned up. The skull was still on top; he rolled it over with his finger and stood up.

Wills looked at Luke. "The other man is there?" He pointed next to the revealed grave.

"Yes, sir."

Wills pulled his knife and poked it into the ground beside the bones. He dug for several minutes and came up with a human rib bone. "Okay, there are two bodies here all right."

Prideux was standing over the burn site with Miles. He was holding the rusted branding iron and studying the head with the OM on it. He held it up as Wills walked toward him. "It's one of their branding irons all right."

Wills looked at it and then scanned the area around them. "I'm satisfied that everything happened as Luke said it did. We have the remains of two bodies, one with a hole in the skull, just as Luke said Bruell finished them off. The branding iron, obviously burnt and long buried, is the clincher. How do you feel about it, Prideux?"

"I see it the same way. I want to see the horses and check those altered brands."

Wills nodded. "I'm pretty sure we'll find them just as Bren said."

They mounted up and rode for Stanford's ranch and the foreman's house where the horse barns were. Pulling up to the foreman's house, they dismounted and looked around. The man Bren and Miles had spoken to earlier walked out of the barn where the older horses were kept. His face showed concern as he approached them. He recognized Miles and Bren.

Prideux stepped forward and pulled back his vest revealing his badge. "U.S. Marshal Prideux. Marshal Wills and I would like to look over those horses you have in the barn."

"Sure." The man's eyes moved from the

marshal to Miles and then Bren. "Is there a problem?"

"Yes, there is. Do you work for a man name of Dillon Stanford?"

"Yes, I'm his foreman. I understand though that he was killed in town today, along with his wife and brother."

"You understand right. Only his name is not Stanford, it's Bruell. He and his brother once ran an outlaw gang on the Natchez Trace. We are investigating his murdering of Owen and Aiden MacMahon eight years ago and stealing their Morgan brood stock. He robbed their bodies of several thousand dollars in the process."

The foreman's eyes grew wide. "Mac-Mahons, he murdered MacMahons? Marshal, that is one hard outfit, I would never deliberately cross them."

Prideux poked his thumb at Miles and Bren. "There's two of them. They come for answers."

The foreman stared at them nervously. "Believe me; I have no knowledge of Stanford's past. I didn't know any of that. I've worked here for the last four years and I only know what Stanford told me."

Miles asked, "Did you ever suspect anything was wrong here?"

The man shook his head. "I never liked

Stanford. He was a weaselly kind of man, but I didn't know that he built this up on robbery and murder, though. I've heard the stories how he treated the businessmen in town, but I have enough of my own problems to deal with so I minded my own business."

"I can understand that."

"If I had known what he did, I wouldn't be here. Now, with him dead I'll have to find another job and a new place for the missus and me to live. So, now I have a new set of problems."

What's your name?"

"Rusty Mitchell."

"Don't go anywhere, Rusty; we'll talk some more later."

Prideux led the way to the open barn door. Rusty moved ahead of them and pointed at the older horses. He haltered the first one and walked it out. Prideux and Wills looked closely at the brand, tracing it with their fingers.

Prideux nodded. "It's altered. The two halves of the 8 don't close together, and they're not the same size, and the bar is just for show."

Wills stepped back. "He must have registered this concocted brand for the purpose of covering the original OM brands."

The marshals had a quick inspection of the other mares and the stud. As they did, Bren went back out to his horse and retrieved the piece of horsehide. They came back to where Miles stood with Luke and Rusty.

Prideux looked at Miles. "The brands were all added to with a cinch ring and a running iron. I'm sure he's had branding irons made up since then with that brand for the cattle and any new horses. I'm also sure if you looked close enough you would see a difference between them and these here on the horses. I'm convinced that Dillon Bruell murdered the MacMahons and started this ranch and town with their horses and money."

Bren held the piece of horsehide hair side out with Stanford's brand facing out for Rusty to see. "Recognize this?"

"It looks like a piece of the horsehide I gave to Ryan. It was from one of the mares I found dead in the stable a few days back."

Bren turned the piece of hide over to the flesh side. Rusty's face fell in distress as he looked at the OM. "I never knew."

Wills addressed Rusty, "Mr. Mitchell, we will be seizing all of Bruell's holdings. You may stay on until there is a formal disposition of the property."

Prideux jerked his head toward Wills to follow him. The two lawmen stepped outside of the barn to talk privately. "Since the horses belong to the MacMahons, they are free to take them. Since this ranch was undoubtedly built up from money stolen from them, the ranch should be signed over to the MacMahons, too. When we get back to Yankton, the judge can put his official stamp on it. That shouldn't be a problem."

Wills considered the idea for several seconds. "I'm agreeable. We'll tell them now and then ride into town where we can write out official paperwork transferring the branded stock and property to the Mac-Mahon family."

They nodded to each other in agreement and returned to the cluster of men waiting inside the barn. "Marshal Wills and I have reached an official decision. The older horses legally belong to the MacMahons; therefore any horses thrown from them are also MacMahon property. In addition to the horses, the property was stocked with cattle and developed with money that was stolen from Owen MacMahon. Marshal Wills and I are transferring the property, and all stock on it, to the MacMahon family. A judge will sign the transfer officially when we get back to Yankton."

Bren and Miles smiled at him. Bren said, "We were sort of hoping you'd see it that way, Marshal."

"Good, it's settled then. You probably want to talk ranch business with Rusty here. We're going back to town to straighten out affairs with the businessmen. See you back at the saloon in a couple hours and we'll put it all to paper."

"We'll be there."

The marshals rode from the property, leaving the four men alone. Miles turned to Rusty. "I'm sorry about the earlier deception, but we had to see those horses and if we had told you the real reason we were here, you might not have let us inspect the horses."

"I have to admit I probably wouldn't have. I might not like Stanford, but I take his wages so I ride for the brand, and I would have protected that brand."

"We appreciate that kind of loyalty. Looks like you've been doing a good job here, Rusty, want to stay on?"

Rusty showed surprise. "Yes, I would. My wife and I live in the house and we like it here. I've put a lot of work into the breeding program for the Morgans, not to mention the cattle. I'd like to continue with it. Stanford never gave me a lick of credit for

291

it, but it was all my work."

"Okay, good. I want to talk to my sister-in-law and nephew up at the main ranch, but I think we'll be keeping this property for the horses and some cattle. In the meantime, you stay on as the ranch manager."

"Manager! Why, thank you."

"How much was Stanford, or I should say Bruell, paying you?"

"Fifty a month, plus the house."

"Fifty! For running the whole place? That sounds like him, though. We'll double that."

Miles then turned his attention to Luke. "Want a job, Luke?"

"I sure do. Things are kind of tight for my ma and sister right now. They do what they can, but I help and right now I'm broke."

"You've got Rusty's old foreman job. Sixty a month work for you?"

Luke's face lit up with excitement. "Yes, sir."

Bren slapped Luke on the back. "A favor done for a MacMahon is never forgotten."

Miles turned back to Rusty. "How many hands do you have on here?"

"Three, besides myself. There's Chuck, Mike, and that kid Jinx, who I can't stand."

"I think we met two of them, and one had to be Jinx. I was ready to blow him out of the saddle."

"Yeah, he has that effect on people. Stanford kept him around because he liked him and gave him special jobs away from the ranch."

"I'll bet he did."

The sound of horses reached them. Rusty looked out the open barn door. "Speak of the devil, there's Mike and Jinx now."

Miles and Bren turned to watch the two as they rode in. Mike was the older man with whom they had spoken to earlier. Dismounting, Jinx swaggered toward Miles and Bren and shouted, "Thought we told you to keep riding."

Miles squared around facing him. The look on his face was cold and deadly.

Rusty grinned at the kid. "Meet the new bosses. Pack your stuff and get out, you're fired."

"What?" The kid's face twisted into a cocky sneer. "You can't fire me; Stanford will have your head." The kid stopped for a second while the rest of what Rusty said sunk in. "What new bosses?"

"New bosses, kid. Stanford is dead, so is his woman and brother. The MacMahons own the place now."

Jinx stared with his mouth opening and closing resembling a fish on dry land. Mike stood several feet behind him. He put his hand over his eyes and shook his head. He knew the name.

"Meet Miles and Bren MacMahon. Hear tell you were trying to run roughshod over them. You're lucky to be alive, you stupid kid."

Miles' expression did not change. "You have three minutes to pack your stuff and get out of here. If you're still here, I'll kill you."

With all the bravado blown out of him, Jinx turned and with the staggering walk of a man hit in the head, the kid headed for the bunkhouse. Mike sighed and turned to follow him.

Miles spoke over his shoulder to Rusty. "Is Mike a good hand?"

"Yeah, he is. He was stuck working with that stupid kid."

Miles called out after him, "Mike, where are you going?"

"To pack up and get out like the kid."

"Why? There's work to do. I want you to work with Rusty and Luke here and put together a complete tally of cattle and property on this ranch. I want to see what we've got and need."

Mike stopped mid-step, his expression filled with surprise. "Yes, sir, right away,

Mr. MacMahon."

"How much was Stanford paying you?"

"Thirty, plus found."

"You'll get a raise, and we'll get a cook in here too."

"Yes, sir, thank you." He grinned. "A real cook would be nice."

"How about Chuck?" Miles asked Rusty. "Is he a good hand?"

"Yes, he's out at the line shack right now."

"Send him word he's still got a job. Rusty, go ahead and get that going here. We're going back to town and taking Luke with us. We have details to work out with the marshals."

Rusty broke into a smile. "Yes, sir. Mind if I tell my wife the good news first?"

"Go right ahead."

As Rusty passed Mike he punched him in the shoulder and they both smiled.

CHAPTER SEVENTEEN

Miles, Bren, and Luke rode back into a Stanfordville that had an entirely different feel to it. There was a festive air with people laughing and talking together. Everything that had the word Stanford on it was already being torn down and thrown into a fire burning at the edge of town. Even the *Stanford's Crystal Queen* sign was gone.

Pulling up beside a man who was tending the fire, Miles commented, "Looks like a celebration in town."

"Yes, sir, there will be a big dance tonight in the town hall and food galore. You boys could be the guests of honor if you stick around. We're also going to have a rechristening of the town. It's our town now and we're going to call it Elkhorn River from here on out."

"Well, we never pass up free food."

"Good, see you there then. A lot of men around here want to buy you a drink."

Miles smiled at him. "And I never pass up free drinks either." They moved on.

They went into the saloon that was formerly the Crystal Queen and found Marshal Prideux and Marshal Wills sitting at a table with papers spread around on the tabletop. Prideux told them to sit down and started shoving papers toward Miles telling him where to sign. He went through the explanations until the last paper was signed. He gave Miles a copy of each and kept a copy for himself.

Prideux raised his hand and the barkeep came over to the table. Prideux looked at him and grinned. "Frank here has taken over the saloon. What did you say you were going to call it again?"

Frank grinned. "I'm calling it the *Miles To Go. S*ort of a play on words for the man who liberated this town from the clutches of Dillon Stanford. I guess his name was actually Bruell, wasn't it?"

Miles grinned. "If it's named after me, do I get free drinks?"

"The first one."

Miles laughed. "Okay, I'll claim my first one and a first one for my friends here."

Frank walked away and came back with a bottle and glasses and filled them. Miles looked at him. "You know, I own a saloon in North Platte, but I don't give myself free drinks either. I'd go broke if I did."

Frank laughed and returned to the bar.

Prideux downed his drink, then dug the sack of Bull Durham out of his pocket and began building a smoke. "Folks are pretty excited around here and you boys seem to be the men of the hour."

Local men were beginning to filter into the saloon. Miles glanced around at them. "I imagine it's like being freed from prison when you were an innocent man all along."

As they talked, a girl in her late teens poked her head in the saloon door and looked around. She slipped in quickly to the table where they sat. Her blonde hair, blue eyes, and pretty face had the attention of every man at the table

"Luke, Ma's been looking all over for you. You've been gone all day." As she spoke to Luke she kept sneaking glances at Bren.

"I've been busy, Sis, I'll explain later. Tell Ma I got a good job."

"Oh, that's wonderful." She tossed another glance at Bren.

Miles leaned in close to Bren and whispered, "Close your mouth, you look like you're simple-minded." Bren snapped his mouth shut but he continued to stare at the girl.

Luke spoke to the men, "This is my sister, Mary." He looked up at her, "Who shouldn't be in a *saloon.*"

Everyone tipped their hats to her and spoke a greeting. She blushed slightly and smiled at them. She then looked directly at Bren. "Luke, there's a dance tonight. Are you staying in town?"

"I didn't know there was one, but I've got work to do."

Miles broke in, "Oh, I think you can start in the morning, Luke."

Miles and the marshals were smiling outright as they watched the locked stares of the girl and Bren. Prideux poked Bren with his elbow. "You'd better ask that pretty girl to the dance before someone else does."

Bren blushed as he stood up. "I'm Bren MacMahon, would you care to go to the dance with me?"

The girl's blue eyes lit up and her fresh face glowed. "I would love to."

"Okay, I will meet you there."

The girl turned and left the room. Luke was grinning at Bren. "She bakes a mighty good berry pie too."

The afternoon waned as the marshals concluded questioning the business owners about Stanford's illegal dealings. There were shop owners who had paid Dillon Stanford three times over for their loans. Those deeds held by Stanford were found in his office and returned to the businessmen. The threat of being burned out or having their shops destroyed kept them paying. Other stories told of Stanford's thugs forcing those who owned their shops to pay for protection so they didn't receive the same treatment as those in debt to him. All in all, the consensus was that Dillon Stanford's death was reason to celebrate.

Miles and Bren, along with Luke, returned to the ranch and met with Rusty and the remaining two hands, Mike and Chuck, whom Rusty had brought in. They were a good crew and Miles was pleased with what he saw in the ranch. Miles told them to take the rest of the day off and head for town to the festivities. That brought smiles all around.

As the crew broke up, Rusty thanked Miles. "In the time I've been here," he told Miles, "I've never seen a dance, picnic, or any kind of town get-together. Stanford was a cruel man who left nothing but misery in his wake."

"It's a sad situation when a man's life breeds nothing but misery around him to such an extent that his death is reason to celebrate."

"There's something to be said for that all right, we're all glad he's gone. His woman, I don't believe they were actually married, and his brother were no better. Having the whole lot of them gone gives this community a rebirth."

"We have been able to settle some matters and answer questions long wondered about for our family too."

"Like your brother?"

Miles nodded. "Him and Aiden, both. Eight years of searching, wondering, and waiting. At least we have our answers."

"Well, I believe we are all better off now. I'm going to tell my wife about the dance and celebration. We haven't had a night out together in years."

"Then, get on out of here and go have a good time."

Rusty looked back over his shoulder and smiled at Miles. "It's going to be from here on out." He walked off toward his house.

Miles glanced at Bren. "I like him."

"I like the whole crew; we got us a good lot with them." He looked at Miles and studied him for several seconds. "You sound like a man that figures to stick around a while."

Miles nodded. "I'm co-owner of the OM

and I've left the running of it to Ita and Cade for too long. It's time for me to take some responsibility and share the burden with them."

"What about your saloon in North Platte?"

"I've been thinking about that. Gandy's done a mighty fine job of running it for me. I think I'll either give it to him or let him run it and I'll be the absentee owner. It'll depend on what he wants to do."

"So, you'll be sticking around?"

"Yeah, especially with a second place to run now."

Bren smiled at him. "Glad to hear that. I don't know about you, but I think it's time to head back into Elkhorn River. The fiddler should be tuning up for that dance."

Miles waved him off. "Go. I ain't much of a dancer; I'll be making my way around talking to folks though."

Bren grinned at him. "That's right, there's a lineup of men wanting to buy you drinks."

"And you have a mighty pretty girl waiting for you. You might want to hit the river first, though, you're smelling a might gamey. Buy a comb and run it through your hair too, it looks like a packrat's nest."

"Thanks, you should look in a mirror sometime yourself."

"I know what I look like, but I don't have a pretty girl waiting for me, so it doesn't matter."

Bren laughed. "See you later you old whiskey-drinking Indian fighter."

Bren arrived at the dance and began looking around for Mary. It was being held in the large empty building that was once intended for community events, that is until Dillon Stanford revealed his true plan and turned the town into a prison. People were milling around moving in and out of the building chatting with each other.

Bren entered the door exchanging nods and greetings with townsfolk. He searched through the crowd looking for Mary and spotted her standing on the side of the main floor against the wall. She was craning her neck trying to see over the crowd and looking for him. They saw each other at the same time. Mary put her arm high in the air and waved at him. He made a beeline across the room toward her.

Several feet from her he stopped and stared. She was only a few years younger than he was. Her blonde hair was pinned up and she was wearing a blue dress that accented her blue eyes. It was a dress probably saved for special occasions, of which there had been few, if any, in this town. She was the prettiest girl he had ever seen. He took a deep breath and moved up to her. They spoke hesitantly, each nervous and excited. The fiddler opened the dance with a fast tune and Bren took her hand.

The dance had been going for an hour. When Bren and Mary weren't dancing they were close to each other talking. The other men recognized Bren as one of the Mac-Mahons who wiped out the Stanfords and, together with the marshals, put their outlaws on the run. No one was willing to butt in between them.

A loud voice slurred with liquor suddenly echoed across the room. The voice held the ominous threat of a man who got ugly and mean when he drank. Such a man could cause havoc in a hurry if he had a gun or was picking fights. The loud ominous voice was coming closer to them. As the drunk got closer, Bren could see it was Jinx.

Mary instantly grew tense and frightened. Bren looked at her. "What's the matter, Mary?"

"Him, he bothers me sometimes. If he sees me in town he approaches me. He even came out to our house once and tried to see me. He drinks and talks mean. He frightens me."

"I know who he is; we fired him off the ranch today. Does Luke know he bothers you?"

She shook her head. "I've never told him. I was afraid Luke would be killed or kill him and go to jail."

Jinx spotted Mary before he recognized Bren. He staggered toward her. "Come on, girl, let's dance."

"I don't want to dance with you. Go away."

Jinx stiffened and scowled, making a mean ugly face. "I said I want to dance, now get on your feet, girl."

Bren stood up, his fists clenched. Jinx stared at him. "Oh, it's the great Mac-Mahon. Maybe I should grovel at your feet."

"Maybe you should leave while you still can. You're drunk and stupid."

By now the room was quiet and everyone was watching. Bren was watching Jinx; however, out of the corner of his eye he could see Luke making his way through the watching crowd, moving toward them.

Jinx took a step to his right in an attempt to get closer to Mary. Bren sidestepped to block him. Jinx glared at him. "I want to dance with my girl."

"She's not your girl. Leave."

Jinx threw an awkward punch at Bren that

missed. Bren slammed a solid fist into Jinx's stomach, doubling him over. He grabbed the drunken man by the back of his collar and drove him head first out the door. He dragged him down the street to a water trough where he pushed Jinx's head in the water. He held him under for several seconds and then pulled him out and threw him backwards so he sprawled out on his back in the street.

Bren leaned down close to him as Jinx sputtered water out of his mouth. "Leave this town and never come back. If I ever hear of you bothering Mary again, I'll make a steer out of you. You understand me?"

Jinx stared up at him, his eyes filled with fear and sudden sobering. He nodded his wet head.

"Now get on your feet, get on your horse, and ride, boy. Don't come back here . . . ever."

Jinx stumbled stupidly to his feet and staggered away down the street away from the community building.

The dance crowd had gathered outside to watch. There were smiles and laughter as the last of Stanford's gang staggered out of their town and their lives. With the fight over, the watchers filed back into the building. As Bren turned back, he saw Luke standing halfway between him and the building.

Luke grinned as Bren approached him. "I figured to back you, but it looks like you took care of it fine."

Bren slapped him on the back. "Thanks for coming along anyway." They headed back to the dance.

Mary was the last one outside the building waiting for him. She smiled and even in the growing darkness he could see how pretty she was. Luke kept on walking and went inside.

Bren stopped in front of her. "We had a little talk; he won't be back or bother you again."

Mary slipped her hand in Bren's. "Thank you." The fiddler struck up a lively tune and the music drifted out the door to them. "Shall we dance some more?"

Bren grinned at her. "It's a dance, isn't it?" Smiling, they went back inside the building.

At the end of the dance Luke met Mary to take her home. She looked up at Bren, "Will I see you again?"

"I plan on being around; after all we have a new ranch to run here."

She stood up on her toes and kissed his cheek. "Thank you again." She left with

Luke, who was laughing under his breath.

Bren was standing still watching them walk away when Miles stepped up and stood beside him. "Just can't keep out of fights, can you?'

"It's one of the things I do best."

"You got that right. Come on; let's get some sleep. We're heading back in the morning."

Chapter Eighteen

Miles and Bren sat on the seat of one of the ranch wagons with a team of the Morgans pulling it. Their saddled horses trailed behind, tied to the back of the wagon. In the bed were two empty pine coffins and a shovel. They pulled up beside the graves that held the last remains of Owen and Aiden MacMahon. Moving the saddle horses, they slid the coffins off the end of the wagon bed and set them on the ground.

It was a solemn occasion and neither man spoke as they dug gently in the dirt of the grave that held Owen. As they found each bone, they placed it in one of the coffins that had been lined with a blanket. When they had retrieved the last bone they folded the blanket over them, closed the lid, and nailed it down. Miles scratched "Owen" on the top with a nail.

They repeated the procedure with the second grave with Miles scratching "Aiden" on the top. Both coffins were lifted back into the wagon bed and tied down. Bren walked over to the spot where the fire had been and picked up the rusted branding iron. He placed it in the bed with the coffins. Returning their horses to the back of the wagon, they sat up on the wagon seat. Miles took up the reins and moved the team toward the road and back to the OM.

The sun inched across the brilliant blue August sky as the wagon moved closer to home. White clouds floated overhead casting shadows on the hills and grasslands as they passed between the sun and earth. Few words were spoken between Miles and Bren during the hours from Elkhorn River to the OM headquarters and home. It was a time of reflection and remembering.

The years of waiting and wondering by the family over the two men loved and lost, and the unending questions of why, and what, were ended. Their emotions were a mix of anger over the actions of Dillon and Arthur Bruell and the satisfaction of knowing that the guilty had not escaped punishment.

The wagon rattling into the yard brought Ita out of the house. Her eyes, locked on the coffins, were filled with questions. Anna and Jo came out behind her and watched from the porch as Ita slowly and hesitantly walked down the steps. Who was in the coffins was written across Ita's face.

Caden walked out slowly; it was evident he was still healing. Rafe came from one of the barns. They came together at the wagon. Ita looked up at Miles as he sat silently on the wagon seat, the reins between his calloused fingers.

"It's Owen and Aiden."

Ita sagged as her eyes welled with tears. She gently placed her hand on the coffin nearest to her. She looked at him, "How? Where?"

"Let's all go in the house and I'll tell you everything." He and Bren climbed off the wagon seat and ushered everyone into the house. Miles looked back at Rafe, who was holding back. "Come on in, Rafe, you're as much a part of this family as anyone." He followed Miles and Bren without a word.

They sat down together in the front room. They were filled with questions, but remained silent. Miles began at the beginning and related finding Stanfordville, and that Dillon and Art were there. He told what the people in the area had said about them. Then, the finding of the horsehide with the altered brand, which led to the ranch, and finding the old Morgans with the altered

311

brands. He told of meeting Luke, who had witnessed the murders and led them to the graves, and the resulting confrontation with Dillon. He told of the marshals' involvement and that the ranch was turned over to them. He left out Art and Kelly's deaths.

Tears rolled down Ita's face, as they did with Anna and Jo. The room remained silent until Anna spoke. "I want to know what happened to Arthur. I want the truth, Miles. I've been buried under a mountain of lies for twenty years and I am sick of lies. I want the truth of Arthur's involvement and what has become of him."

Miles looked at her, hesitant to tell. "Okay, the truth. I had already killed Dillon. I met Bren and Luke at the saloon where the Stanfords kept their office. We went in and Art and Kelly, who you knew as Maude, were there. The marshals came in behind us and it was the first we learned of them actually being Bruells rather than Stanfords. Kelly got scared and began to tell everything that had happened. She said that Art had wired Dillon that two men had bought the horses and were headed back here, that they should steal the horses when they came through. They did. Owen and Aiden chased them and were ambushed and murdered. She also said Art was the one that shot Cade." He paused, looking uncomfortable.

Anna was weeping openly. "So Art had been in contact with Dillon prior to this and I never knew. Please Miles . . . please tell me all."

"Art kept shouting at Kelly to shut up, and when she didn't . . . he shot her. Then, the marshal . . . shot Art. He's dead."

Anna's face was wet with tears and twisted in anguish. She looked at Ita. "I'm so sorry Ita . . . so sorry."

Ita shook her head. "It's not your fault."

The room remained silent with only the sounds of Anna's sobs. Miles stood up. "I think we should bury them on the hill where you watched everyday for them, Ita."

Ita nodded. "Yes, that would be fine."

They left the house and followed the wagon up to the hilltop. The men dug two graves in the soft soil and lowered the coffins. Words were said over them and then the heavy sound of dirt thumping on the almost hollow boxes was the final answer to eight years of questions.

Miles drove the wagon back to the barn. Jo walked down arm-in-arm with Caden. She left him at the house and went inside. Caden, Bren, and Rafe joined together at the corral. They stood in silence for several minutes and watched Ita standing at the foot of the graves and Anna standing like a silent sentinel beside her friend.

Rafe coughed to clear his voice. "She watched from that hill for eight years never giving up hope. Now, she knows. I wonder if it's better knowing for sure or if it's better to always have hope."

Caden kept his eyes on the hill and shrugged. "I don't know. I think she always knew, but admitting it was too much like closing the book on them. Now, it's settled for certain, even though it's painful. Yeah, I think that's worth something."

Ita turned toward Anna. "At least they're home."

"I'm so sorry, Ita. If not for Arthur this would have never happened, had he not been such an evil man. I am afraid having me in your home will be a constant reminder of him and I should leave."

"No, you should not leave. Where would you go? Back to that house with all of the bad memories? To live your life alone because of him? You know it's just a matter of time before Caden and Jo are married and they will be building their own home here on the OM. What are you going to do there all alone?"

"But, what he did . . ."

314

"Yes, what *he* did, not you. *He* did it, and you have suffered enough because of him. Besides, I could use a friend around here."

Anna smiled through her tears. "Are you sure?"

"Positive." The two women embraced and then walked down the hill toward the house.

Rafe pointed up the hill at them. "Looks like things are all right there." He turned and went back to his work.

Caden spoke to his brother. "What really happened when Miles killed Dillon Bruell? I'm sure he lightened it up for the sake of Anna and Jo."

"What he told me was that he confronted Dillon in the livery and Dillon laughed at him. He said we could never prove anything, never prove who the bones really belonged to, and he would walk away a free man. Even with Luke's testimony, it was his word against Dillon's and Luke was a kid at the time. Miles knew that might be true . . . that we might not be able to prove the murders in court. The stolen horses, yes, the murders, no. The horses were the least of it. Miles said he considered what Dillon had done, how he cold-bloodedly murdered Pa and Aiden for seven horses. How he had buried them and hid his crime. He thought of how the stolen money off their dead

315

bodies had built Dillon's criminal empire.

"Dillon knew he could walk away and laughed about it. Miles considered the outlaw gang Dillon was running and the murders and robbery still happening because of that man and the danger he was inflicting on the people around there. Then there were the decent townspeople and the misery they suffered trapped in Dillon's spiderweb of fear. All of that was because of one wretched man. He knew Dillon could walk away to continue his criminal rampage. He wasn't about to let that happen."

Caden looked back up at the hill with the fresh graves. "So, he called in the jury of six."

"Yeah. He said Dillon was too evil to live."

Miles walked up to them leading his saddled horse. "How are you doing, Cade? See you're up and around."

Caden grinned at him. "Can't keep a MacMahon down for long."

Miles lifted his chin toward the hill. "Well, that's settled. We got Dillon and Art, but I guess George and Ed are still on the loose."

"Ed is anyway."

Miles raised an eyebrow at him. "Oh? You're not telling something."

"George Bruell was the George Carson who worked for us."

"No. You're joking. He was under our noses all the time?"

"Sam and Carl started seeing some things in Randy's death that didn't line up with the story George had told. Carl had Randy's rifle and it had an empty shell in the chamber and was down a couple in the magazine. They got to figuring it was Randy who actually shot the rustler and not George, which meant he lied. Sam realized that Randy had been shot in the back and that left only one person who could have done it. We confronted him, set up a little trap, and he walked right into it. He admitted to killing Randy, and that he was George Bruell."

"Where is he now?"

"Where do you think?"

"Coyote and buzzard bait."

Caden nodded. "We strung him up."

"And Ed?"

Caden shrugged. "Still running probably. He was the one you almost hung when we caught up with the rustlers. The one George couldn't remember."

"I thought he knew George a little too well. I was having my own suspicions about George the last couple of days. I was going to bring it up to you, but it looks like you took care of it the MacMahon way."

Miles told Caden about the new ranch

and the crew. They would ride down and show Rusty and Luke how to run the ranch the MacMahon way.

"It sounds like you have plans to stay around for a while, so what's up with the saddled horse? You look like you're leaving again."

"I have to take care of my business in North Platte. I've still got a couple hours of daylight left so I figured to use them. I've left the burden of running this place on you and Ita long enough, I'll be back."

"We'll be glad to have you permanently home."

Miles poked Bren with his elbow. "Want to ride along to North Platte?"

"Well, actually, I was figuring on riding back to give Rusty and Luke a hand with the new place."

Miles grinned at him. "A certain pretty little blonde-haired girl wouldn't be playing any part in this decision, would it?"

"Well, maybe a little."

Miles laughed. "Maybe a whole lot." He put his hand out to Bren. "And you said there was no excitement left in the west."

Bren shook his hand. "Go on, you old whiskey-drinking Indian fighter."

Miles shook Caden's hand. "I'll be back." He stepped into the saddle and rode out.

Caden looked at his brother. "So, tell me about this blonde-haired girl."

"Sure, big brother, let's get a cup of coffee and I'll tell you all about it."

The two brothers walked toward the house together as the summer sun inched its way toward the western horizon. The eastern side of the hills were in shadow while the peaks continued to reflect the heat of the day. For the first time in eight years, Ita MacMahon did not climb the hill to watch and hope. Her men were home, if only to sleep in the earth of their own land.

ABOUT THE AUTHOR

Dave P. Fisher is a writer of western novels, western short stories, and outdoor nonfiction articles with over four hundred works published, including thirteen western novels and books and over sixty short stories. Dave's accomplishments and credits include winning two *Will Rogers Medallion Awards,* one each for Western Fiction and Western Humor. He has won eight People's Choice Awards for western short stories and has been included in fifteen anthologies.

His outdoor and western writing is steeped in historical accuracy, drawing on extensive research and his personal background as a lifetime Westerner, working cowboy, horse packer, and guide.

You can learn more about Dave's background and writing at his website: www .davepfisher.com.

The employees of Thorndike Press hope you have enjoyed this Large Print book. All our Thorndike, Wheeler, and Kennebec Large Print titles are designed for easy reading, and all our books are made to last. Other Thorndike Press Large Print books are available at your library, through selected bookstores, or directly from us.

For information about titles, please call:
  (800) 223-1244

or visit our Web site at:
  http://gale.cengage.com/thorndike

To share your comments, please write:
  Publisher
  Thorndike Press
  10 Water St., Suite 310
  Waterville, ME 04901